HOUSES IN THE LANDSCAPE

other books by John Penoyre

Observer's Book of Architecture
 (with Michael Ryan)

HOUSES IN THE LANDSCAPE

A Regional Study of Vernacular Building
Styles in England and Wales

John and Jane Penoyre

with illustrations by the authors

faber and faber
LONDON · BOSTON

First published in 1978
by Faber and Faber Limited
3 Queen Square London WC1
First published in Faber Paperbacks in 1984
Printed in Great Britain by
BAS Printers Limited, Over Wallop, Hampshire
All rights reserved

British Library Cataloguing in Publication Data

Penoyre, John
   Houses in the landscape.
   1. Architecture, Domestic—England
   2. Vernacular architecture—England
   I. Title   II. Penoyre, Jane
   728.3'0942   NA7328

   ISBN 0-571-13287-1

Contents

Maps

Regional Boundaries

SE	South-eastern counties	WC	West-central counties
SW	South-western counties	EC	East-central counties
D+C	Devon and Cornwall	NC	North-central counties
EA	East Anglia	N	Northern England
SC	South-central counties	W	Wales

Introduction

It is not always appreciated quite what a wealth of variety and interest lies in the simple and unassuming buildings of the countryside.

This book describes the different regional domestic building styles in England and Wales. Local building styles and techniques are found principally in the humbler buildings whose builders have been only minimally influenced by outside fashions and have only used materials immediately to hand. Such buildings, using local techniques and local materials, are said to be in the vernacular and are genuinely indigenous to their soil.

That definition confines our study almost entirely to small farmhouses and cottages. It automatically excludes fashionable Georgian houses, conforming to universal eighteenth-century ideas of symmetry and good taste, as well as Victorian buildings that often relied upon pattern books for their design and upon alien materials carried in on the railways and canals for their construction. We have, however, occasionally referred to such buildings in districts where there are no earlier houses and where the Georgian and Victorian aesthetic has been modified by the introduction of local features and materials. There are also innumerable simple eighteenth- and nineteenth-century buildings, for the most part modest labourer's cottages, which owe little to pattern books or nation-wide concepts of design and are very real examples of a local style. In the description that follows, a good deal of space is devoted to local building materials because in these simple buildings the available materials are the principal dictators of style.

Throughout the book we have used the term cottage in the general sense of a very small house. It is however as well to remember that many of the earlier small farmhouses were converted after the eighteenth- and nineteenth-century en-closures into two or three dwellings for farm labourers. (Previously the many smaller farmers housed their relatively few hired labourers literally under their roof in the attics.) So what we have for simplicity often called 'a pair of cottages' might more correctly be described as a converted farmhouse.

Most buildings have been altered at some time during their life, adapting to the changing needs of the generations. Changes and additions are carried out in the spirit of their age; so Victorian extensions or Georgian façades often convert genu-inely vernacular buildings, particularly farmhouses, into a dull conformity, while many twentieth-century alterations seem more concerned with convenience than appearance.

Bearing these matters in mind, it has remained for us to make a choice of examples, avoiding the grand and fashionable and the non-typical, the poorly converted and the imitation. That is not always easy and in the end we have had to rely upon personal taste. We have chosen to illustrate what we like and what we believe to represent some positive aspect of the spirit of the region under review.

We have had to recognise that a book of this sort must be limited in its scope and have therefore excluded reference to urban or suburban localities, although these have distinctive vernacular styles of their own. We have also reluctantly excluded all the beautiful barns, byres, mills, oast-houses and other similar buildings that contribute so much in their direct functional simplicity and generous proportions to the architecture of the countryside.

For convenience, we have divided the country into regions,

some large and some smaller according to where the centres of powerful vernacular influence seem to lie or according to generally recognised geographical concepts, such as East Anglia. Regions must be defined and for simplicity we have chosen to use county boundaries, even if these are quite artificial, for of course one regional style merges more or less gradually into the next.

Some counties straddle the regional boundaries and are transitional in their building styles, so their allocation to one or other of the adjacent regions is more or less arbitrary. Hertfordshire is a case in point: to the north and east of the county its buildings are East Anglian in character whereas along its western half the traditions of Buckinghamshire predominate.

The comparatively recent industrial and commercial development around the West Midlands, Greater Manchester and the coalfields of central England has led to the swamping of vernacular styles in these areas under the relentless tide of later buildings, whereas in areas where the slower pace of agricultural life has continued uninterrupted, and particularly areas that enjoyed a large measure of prosperity in former times, such as the Cotswolds, very many buildings with a splendid vernacular tradition are preserved. Inevitably, greater emphasis has been given to the latter.

We hope that the wide variety and interest of vernacular buildings will be appreciated for their own sake. But the book may also be used for reference, more particularly to those characteristics that seem relevant to modern domestic developments, and to encourage anyone concerned with such buildings to identify what it is that gives localities their architectural flavour.

This might read as though we were advocating traditional designs for new buildings, but that is most emphatically not so and would be a formula for certain disaster. The scale of modern buildings demanded by modern needs and modern building regulations makes any attempt at reproducing old cottage designs quite meaningless. Architecture is the outcome of social needs, economic pressures and the skill of those who design and build. Economic pressures inevitably demand that the materials used are those most readily obtainable; social needs demand buildings of a different layout to those built in the past; and modern techniques make available other and more economical methods. Nevertheless, within the limitations of economy and the scope of contemporary needs and techniques there remain many choices open to the designer: to vary the roof shape, to use materials in a way that harmonises rather than creates a discord with local character, and to respect the scale and proportions, the colours and traditions of the locality.

We have not attempted an historical survey nor have we attempted to trace the development of the house from its beginnings to the present day. Our book is essentially a regional review of the outward appearances of buildings, and for this reason is largely a picture-book with descriptions of each region.

Passing reference has been made throughout to the general characteristics of the landscape and its vegetation. Regional building styles cannot be separated from their backgrounds, for to uproot a building style from the environment that created it would be meaningless and it is essential for a true appreciation of vernacular buildings to think of them in their proper physical context.

The sketch maps that go with each region show the geology and the main distribution of the principal building materials. The areas showing the various materials cannot be regarded as precisely defined with hard and fast boundaries but are a good indication of the main zones of occurrence. They have been derived from observation and from a map of England and Wales on which we have plotted over a thousand examples taken from photographs, of which a small selection is printed in the book.

The photographs themselves are snapshots taken from the highway of any and all buildings we saw that appealed to us as being at once attractive, genuinely vernacular in style and typical of their area. We hope very much that the various owners will not be offended at seeing a picture of their house in print. It would have been polite and informative as well as pleasant to have talked to all householders rather than only those we were fortunate enough to meet but alas, time, the universal enemy, made that absolutely impossible. The quality of the photographs, which were taken at all seasons, in all weathers and at all times of day, may leave something to be desired in some cases. We have nevertheless thought it worth while to include them all as illustrative of the points we are making.

Nearly all the line drawings in the text are idealised portraits of real buildings, although some are intended as pure diagrams.

We would of course like to acknowledge the debt we owe to the authors of the numerous books we have referred to during the preparation of the text. No study of this sort can hope to be an entirely original work, but inevitably relies to a large extent upon the researches and hard work of others in the field.

Of the many books which we have read we would like particularly to acknowledge our debt to Alec Clifton-Taylor for his book *The Pattern of English Building* and to R. W. Brunskill for his *Illustrated Handbook of Vernacular Architecture*. Earlier works, too numerous to mention here, have proved of great value, but perhaps none more so than Sydney Jones's books on various regional styles which he has illustrated with such charming drawings. A very brief bibliography is given at the end of the book as a guide to further reading.

The idea for undertaking this study sprang from a deep affection for the countryside and its buildings and has led us along a path more absorbing and rewarding even than we had expected.

We trust that the book will help to stimulate in others a similar interest and affection.

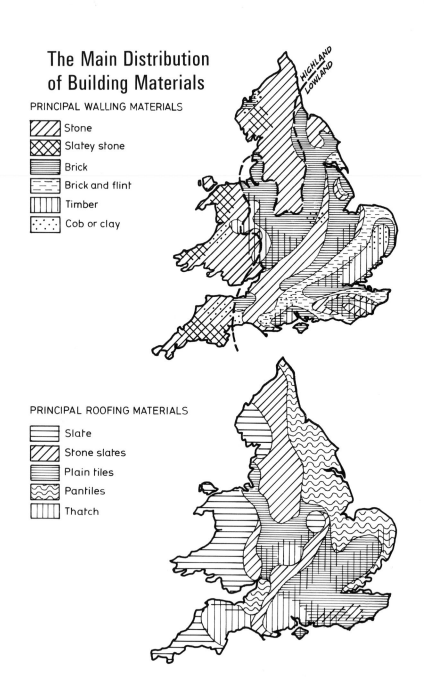

The Main Distribution of Building Materials

HIGHLAND
LOWLAND

PRINCIPAL WALLING MATERIALS

- Stone
- Slatey stone
- Brick
- Brick and flint
- Timber
- Cob or clay

PRINCIPAL ROOFING MATERIALS

- Slate
- Stone slates
- Plain tiles
- Pantiles
- Thatch

1. Local Differences

Differences in styles of building are caused by differences in Time and Place.

Apart from minor regional time-lags, at any one time buildings all over the country have characteristics in common that spring from a similarly advanced technology, a similarity of social need and a general acceptance of what is contemporarily considered appropriate. For instance, we can broadly say that, regardless of location, by the seventeenth century all but the most primitive houses had chimneys, or that by the eighteenth century glass in reasonable-sized panes was universally available. Similarly, superior roof construction techniques and increased prosperity enabled buildings in the eighteenth century to be deeper, back to front, than their predecessors, a circumstance that lends buildings of this date an unmistakable generosity of proportion. These are differences of Time attributable to nation-wide changes of fashion, technology and social habit.

Conversely, such traditional building characteristics as derive from Place are relatively uninfluenced by their date. These are the characteristics brought about by the available materials, the local climate and local skills and needs.

This is a regional review, not an historical one, as we have said, and consequently the emphasis is on the effects of Place rather than those of Time. That is not to say that the effects of history are less important in moulding the local character of buildings; indeed, the period during which a district developed and its subsequent history of progress, decline or stagnation will profoundly influence the particular regional character of what remains to be seen to-day. Thus, the rich farm lands of the Suffolk-Essex border were developed early and have suffered no great onslaught of progress in recent centuries; consequently the buildings in the area exhibit all the notable characteristics of the immediate post-medieval period. By contrast, the buildings of the Lincolnshire peat fens, not effectively drained until the nineteenth century, or those of the Durham coalfields, swamped by industrial activity, are predominantly nineteenth-century in character and, because of their use of imported materials and their pattern-book designs, few buildings in such areas can qualify as vernacular.

The question that considerations of this sort immediately raise is why one region was rich and another poor, the one developed hundreds of years ago, the other only recently. The answer goes back to the basic geology of the country.

Geology plays a fundamental part in determining all aspects of human existence. The type of rock and the regional topography it creates will determine whether a community is rich or poor, what vegetation flourishes, whether it is forested or barren and how many people the land will support. Geology provides the materials for their homes and is the principal factor in establishing regional building styles.

The two factors of Time and Place do however constantly interact and cannot be separated. For example, throughout the Jurassic limestone belt, for many centuries wealth has been derived from sheep-raising and quarrying. These open limestone uplands stretch north-eastwards from the Purbeck hills in Dorset to the Yorkshire coast and all along this line broadly similar stone-building techniques are used. Period style however varies in different localities according to the different times when profits from wool and stone first created enough wealth for small houses to be built of permanent materials, and there is no doubt that period building style profoundly influenced the appearance of the buildings and the architectural character of the various regions traversed by the same limestone. Again the differences in date at which broadly similar localities flourish are caused by such factors as the distance from centres of commerce and the suitability of local products to their contemporary markets.

Few geological formations, although shown as one colour on the Ordnance map, provide consistent building materials throughout their range. This is because geological classification is based on the age of the formation and not on the physical properties of the rocks and soils it yields. In contrast to the relatively consistent Jurassic limestone formation, the Greensand yields sands, hard grey ragstone, soft Bargate sandstone, hot brown ironstones and even the strange chocolate-bar Carstones of north-west Norfolk. Similarly, the Chalk not only provides soft white chalk-stone from its lower strata and abundant flints which are used for walling wherever the formation occurs, but also, in limited areas—by some fluke of sedimentation—a mixture of chalk and clay which sets hard enough to use in a moulded walling technique called wichert. Superficial deposits of alluvium and the effects of glaciation frequently obscure the underlying rocks, giving rise to oak forests or the presence of brick clays in areas which appear from the map to be likely to yield building stone.

So reference to the geological map is not alone enough to determine what the local building material will be.

England and Wales can be divided into two main zones, highland and lowland. Highland areas lie to the west and north of a line embracing the extreme south-west of the country, Wales, the Pennines and the North of England. To the south and east of this line lies lowland England.

As a broad generalisation we can say that buildings in the highland areas are likely to be built of hard intractable stone and those in lowland areas of softer more easily worked stone, of timber or of brick. We can also generalise further to say that the lowland areas are richer than the highland, and that we can therefore expect buildings to be more modest in the latter.

This simplistic model, based on the geological and agricultural origins of the regions, has been considerably upset by historical and economic factors, such as the prosperity created by the late medieval wool trade (which enabled wealth to be created from agriculturally poor soil), by industrialisation and by the intensive exploitation of mineral resources during the last two centuries, so that the true pattern is far more complicated.

In addition, in most valley areas, whether in the lowland or highland zones, we can expect traditional buildings of timber to predominate (provided the areas were developed before the practice of building in timber was abandoned) and we can expect the presence of brick-clays to produce a strong local tradition of brickwork and clay tiling wherever it occurs in association with an adequate fuel supply. Where building stone is poor or hard to come by and there is no timber for either fuel or construction, buildings must be of cob—compacted earth and clay.

In highland Britain, the rocks which are used for building may be sedimentary, metamorphic or igneous. In lowland England, the many fine building stones are all of sedimentary origin. The limestones and the products of the Greensand and the Chalk have been mentioned.

Enough has been said to emphasise that England and Wales are packed with geological variety. In the British Isles the nature of the rocks changes every few miles, each having its effect on the landscape, on how people live and on what buildings they erect.

The main intention of our book, then, is to highlight the differences in the external appearance of traditional domestic buildings in the various regions. Fascinating though it may be to attempt to follow the reasons for local differences in style in all their complexity, we have concentrated on visual results rather than causes and we have made little more than passing reference to physical and social origins. We do, however, give some account of local geology, as we have said, because this seems of over-riding importance for setting the house truly in its landscape.

2. South-Eastern Counties

Surrey, Sussex and Kent

Timber, Hung Tiles and Weatherboarding

The South-Eastern counties of Surrey, Sussex and Kent have a complicated geology and consequently the building types within the region vary considerably in detail. In spite of this, the region as a whole has a distinctive architectural character quite different from that of its neighbours. In the great bowl of the Weald, colours and forms are bright and cheerful to match the prosperous and smiling landscape of its hopfields, its orchards and its oasts. Here, brown, red and brilliant orange tiles, white painted weatherboarding and red bricks combine with the huge slopes of plain-tiled roofs, sweeping almost to the ground, to make a picture of warmth and well-being scarcely to be matched elsewhere in England. The buildings of the chalk uplands are simpler and more austere as suits their wider skies and open landscape.

The main geographical feature of the region is the Weald, surrounded on three sides by chalk hills. Beyond the downs to the north lie the levels of the Thames estuary; to the south lies the open sea. The Weald was once a land of dense woods and swampy clay valleys and consequently timber and brick predominate as basic building materials, although the Greensand ridges and the older hills of the High Weald provide some excellent building stones.

The Weald has been an area of iron-smelting since Saxon times and before, the industry owing its long history of success to the combined presence of the ore, of the fuel in the form of the

South-Eastern Counties

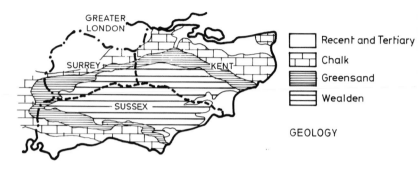

Recent and Tertiary
Chalk
Greensand
Wealden

GEOLOGY

GREATER LONDON
SURREY
KENT
SUSSEX

Brick
Flint
Timber
Stone

PRINCIPAL WALLING
MATERIALS

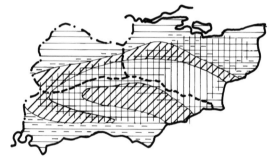

Weatherboarding
Hung tiles

PRINCIPAL CLADDING
MATERIALS

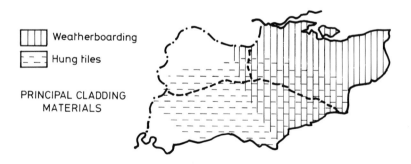

dense oak forests of the region and of the power provided by the numerous small streams.

First the Saxons and later the Normans cleared the forests for charcoal, for pasture and later for settled farm holdings, for the landlords often combined the activities of farming and smelting. By the system of inheritance in this part of England, property was left to all the children and not to the eldest alone, and this factor may well have contributed to the great number of prosperous small farms and early manor houses in the area. Kent and Sussex produce some of the best examples of late medieval yeomen's hall houses in the country.

Hall houses are the descendants of the sort of house built in Saxon and early medieval times comprising one huge room, the hall, in which all activities took place. This sort of simple but rather grand house was later developed with kitchens and a buttery with a gallery over at one end and a dais and later an upstairs room for the family at the other. So almost all hall houses have three main parts, the hall itself in the middle and at either end a two-storeyed element, the first floor being jettied out beyond the ground storey. In this part of England all three elements are covered with a single huge fully hipped roof, originally thatched and now tiled. It is a feature peculiar to the Wealden hall house, as are the resulting deep eaves in the central part between the jetties, supported on highly characteristic curved timber brackets [9]. Elsewhere, as in East Anglia, the two-storey elements are separately roofed. The later introduction of a chimney allowed a first floor to be built over the hall and practically all hall houses to-day are dominated by a huge chimney.

These early timber houses, built mostly in the ostentatious age of the Tudors, made of oak on a low plinth of brick or stone, were built with a reckless excess of vertical timbers, the plaster-filled spaces between the uprights being scarcely wider than the timbers themselves. Their owners liked the rich texture of the closely spaced timbers which gratified their wish for display. As time passed and timber became scarcer due to the inroads of the charcoal burners and the farmers, and as the fashions became

A Kentish hall house

more modest, the uprights of the frame were spaced further and further apart until, by the seventeenth and eighteenth centuries, the densely spaced cage of timbers had been replaced by a wide-open frame, usually infilled with bricks [8, 11]. As the bricks had no structural function, they were often laid in random patterns.

When tile making became more general, towards the end of the seventeenth century, many buildings were faced with hung tiles, more particularly on their gable ends and the sides exposed to the weather, for the brick and plaster infillings were not entirely weatherproof. Some buildings have brick and stone ground

Stone ground floor, timber first floor

floors and timber first floors and are tiled only on their upper storeys [5]. Very many of the houses of the area to-day have this division of materials between the ground and first floors.

Imported softwood, which became available during the eighteenth century, was an alternative facing material that became extremely popular in Kent, and indeed, white-painted weatherboarding is to-day the hall-mark of the Kentish scene, so universal is its use [1]. Previously, untreated or tarred elm boarding had been used, but there are not many examples left to-day. More often than not, older houses that were built wholly of

Kentish weatherboarding

timber were re-faced with weatherboarding from the eaves to the ground, but, as in the case of tiling, houses built with a brick or stone ground floor were weatherboarded at first-floor level. Farm buildings were often tarred but most weatherboarding to-day is painted white. In contrast, window frames are usually painted black, outlining the windows, while the opening casements and glazing bars remain white. This imparts a crisp appearance to the houses which is characteristic of Kent and East Sussex [3]. There is also a good tradition of eighteenth- and nineteenth-century weatherboarded cottages which can be seen in Surrey towns and some London suburbs [4].

But for the region as a whole, the plain tile remains the most characteristic and generally used material, both as hung tiles and in the vast sweeps of roof which run down in the typical 'cat-slides' of this part of England [12].

The plain tile is about ten inches by six (250 mm × 150 mm), with minor variations according to date and locality, and is slightly curved or whale-backed so that the bottom edge of each tile lies hard against the one below. Tiles are laid to overlap three-deep so that only about four inches (100 mm) show. Modern tiles have a hooked top end for hooking over the battens and are usually only nailed every third or fourth course, but older tiles were made without the hooks and were pegged at every course, usually with oak pegs hooked over the tiling battens. All the older tiles distort slightly when burnt in the kiln and these small irregularities, together with the slight curve of the tile, give the plain tiled roofs of the south-east of England their rich texture. The lichens and mosses that grow on the roofs modify their reds to browns and yellows, whereas the vertical hung tiles, being dryer, retain the brilliant orangey-red of their firing [6].

Kentish tile-hanging

Early hung tiles are always rectangular; later, particularly in the nineteenth century, 'fish-scales' and other shaped tiles were often worked into patterns or stripes on the elevation and add considerable variety to the texture [7]. Taking the hung tiles round a corner presents a problem to the tiler and in this part of the country corners are either finished with a stout vertical timber batten, splayed out at the bottom, against which the tiles are butted, or in later examples specially shaped angle tiles are used. This is less satisfactory as it is difficult to make the angled 'specials' match the tiles in colour. Window and door frames in tile-hung walls are built flush with the tile face to allow the tiles to butt against them without difficult corners.

An ingenious type of hung tile, the mathematical tile, was invented in the eighteenth century to imitate brickwork, a fashion that was given some impetus by the Brick Taxes in the latter part of the century. Brick elevations were fashionable and accorded well with the Georgian sophistication of the South-east towns, and many of the older houses were built of timber and needed facings to preserve them from the weather. The mathematical tile, which is specially shaped so that it presents a flat surface rather than an overlapping appearance, was often black-glazed and the resulting shiny black elevations are a feature of many prosperous southern towns. The absence of lintels and arches over the windows and doors, together with a certain wavyness of surface, gives the clue to their identity, as does the presence of the corner battens.

Mathematical tiles

Good building stones are not common in these counties, but where they do occur they have strong local differences. Sandstones of the Wealden hills and the Greensand belts are yellow, brown and grey or even greenish-white. They are used rather coarsely squared, mostly in older houses. Nineteenth-century examples often combine stone with brick corners and edges to windows and doors [14]. In parts of Surrey there occurs a dark ironstone known as Carstone, and small chips of this blackish brown rock are used to decorate the joints between the stones of the buildings, a practice known as garnetting or galletting. Garnetting mostly appears on the Greensand ridge between Guildford and Sevenoaks. Further east along the ridge the tradition is continued, using chips of Kentish ragstone as an alternative to ironstone. Ragstone is a hard form of Greensand stone found in the Maidstone area, grey in colour and very hard to work, and it is therefore more often used for rubble walling than as squared stones. It was popular with Victorian ecclesiastical architects.

Stone roofing slates were quarried in the Weald from the seventeenth century onwards, more particularly in the areas around Horsham and Tunbridge Wells. They are massively heavy and fine in character, suitable only for simple gable roofs, and are usually laid at a 45° pitch [10, 15]. This is lower than the average plain tile pitch, which is between 50° and 55°.

Stone tiles on a Sussex farm

It is generally thought that plain tiles for roofing were derived from the oak shingles used extensively in the Middle Ages in this part of England. Early plain tiled roofs were often fully hipped, as in the yeomen's hall houses, but the common type of tiled roof throughout the area is half-hipped [7]. That gives a part-gable at the end of the house which can take a window to light the roof space, for dormer windows were not much used traditionally in this region. This half-hip, sometimes combined with a small gablet at the ridge, is probably a copy of the earlier thatched roof, where a half-hip at the end of the building was more weather-proof than a straw gable.

Compared with their Wealden counterparts, the buildings of the chalk uplands have little charm or romance and are for the most part undistinguished. Apart from older buildings in the valley bottoms, the chalk uplands seem not to have been developed until the late eighteenth or nineteenth centuries. As in other chalk downlands of England, brick and flints provide most of the walling materials. The cottages therefore have similar characteristics to those in other chalk areas, like north Norfolk; the flint, being difficult to lay to a true angle, is practically always faced with brickwork at the corners and at the jambs of windows and doors [15]. Plinths, string courses and a two- or three-course cornice beneath the eaves and at the verges are always of brick. Pebbles from the beach are sometimes used in coastal areas near the downs, again with brick angles and jambs.

The use of flint pebbles which can be got from the beach, all of the same shape and size, appealed particularly to eighteenth-century taste, and neatly coursed pebble walls, with exactly similar round stones arranged in precise rows, often tarred or painted but sometimes left in their natural blue-grey, are a striking and attractive feature of any southern coastal town with a claim to fashion.

Roofs in chalk districts are either of plain tiles or slates, for slates were popular in the late eighteenth and nineteenth centuries because they were cheaper and needed less robust timbers to support them. Pantiles, so conspicuous a feature of the east coast north of the Thames estuary, are seldom used in the area and are certainly not typical.

Bricks have for long been an important product of the Thames estuary and of the Weald. In the latter locality, the bricks are brown or red, often brindled. Around Sittingbourne and Faversham the clays from the chalky soils of the estuary bake to a bright yellow or, when overburnt, to a dark purple. They are the famous London 'stocks' which for two hundred years or more have contributed towards the London scene.

Further east, beyond Canterbury, there are many old brick houses, mostly of brownish bricks [16]. These houses reflect the influence of the Low Countries in their occasional stepped or Dutch gables and in the fine quality of their early brickwork.

As for the general shape of buildings, this varies with locality. Kentish farmhouses are mostly of a simple, rather long, rectangular shape, with a half-hipped roof dominated by a large central chimney stack [2]. In the west of the region, farmhouses are more complicated in form, with minor gables and lean-to roofs, although the half-hipped main roof with a central chimney still dominates in earlier houses [12]. Most nineteenth-century cottages however follow the simple two-storeyed form seen throughout the country, with small chimneys at each end of the gabled or hipped roof [6]. Single-storeyed cottages are not common, although they can be seen on Romney Marsh.

A Sussex farmhouse

Comparing the buildings of these South-eastern counties with those of East Anglia, it is interesting to find the vernacular styles so different in spite of the superficial similarity between the richly timbered farming country of Suffolk and that of the Weald. Admittedly, the weatherboarded houses of Essex are very like those of Kent (although the former for some reason are more often painted black), but the earlier type of Suffolk house, plastered and colour-washed all over, tall and complicated in

1

2

3

4

SOUTH-EASTERN COUNTIES

1 Tenterden, KENT. A weatherboarded alley (*page 27*)
2 Near Groombridge, EAST SUSSEX. A large weatherboarded farmhouse with a central chimney and a plain tiled roof (*page 32*)
3 Rye, EAST SUSSEX. Eighteenth-century weatherboarding painted white, with black window frames (*page 27*)
4 Leatherhead, SURREY. Nineteenth-century weatherboarded semi-detached cottages (*page 27*)

5

6

7

8

SOUTH-EASTERN COUNTIES

5 Burwash, EAST SUSSEX. Tile-hung first floors (*page 27*)

6 Newdigate, SURREY. A cottage with bright-coloured tile-hanging (*pages 28 & 32*)

7 Ham Street, KENT. A typical small Kentish farmhouse with fish-scale tile-hanging (*pages 28 & 30*)

8 Bletchingley, SURREY. A timber-framed house with brick infill panels and jettied first floor (*page 26*)

9

10

11

12

SOUTH-EASTERN COUNTIES

9 Iden Green, KENT. A typical early Kentish yeoman's farmhouse, with close timbering, jetties and a fully hipped roof (*page 25*)

10 Slinfold, SURREY. Horsham stone slates on a plain-shaped roof (*page 30*)

11 Ockley, SURREY. Brick and half-timbering: a typical Surrey combination (*page 26*)

12 Westerham, KENT. Irregular roofs and cat-slides in plain tiling (*pages 27 & 32*)

13

14

15

16

SOUTH-EASTERN COUNTIES

13 Near Trottiscliffe, KENT. Brown ironstone blocks with garnetted joints (*pages 29 & 30*)
14 Amberley, WEST SUSSEX. Greensand combined with brick and thatch (*page 29*)
15 Steyning, WEST SUSSEX. Brick and flint cottages with a noble roof of large sandstone slates (*pages 30 & 31*)
16 Wingham, KENT. Villages in this part of east Kent are mostly built of brick because of Dutch influence (*page 32*)

form, has no equivalent in the south east, nor is there much tile-hanging in East Anglia. There is of course little or no building stone in East Anglia, but there is plenty of brick clay and chalk for making lime in both these areas; yet the styles of building are quite different.

It seems that groups of people who settle different regions, in spite of their broadly similar continental origins and of the similarity of their basic building materials, will still create individual building styles if communications between the two are poor. In this case, the Thames estuary would have been something of a barrier with its mud flats and treacherous currents.

How different were the Danes and the Anglo-Saxons, and did the differences in their racial characteristics or temperaments persist so far into recent times as to influence the sort of buildings which these people liked to put up and which are still standing to-day? One likes to imagine the inhabitants of Suffolk being more at home with the softer materials of wet plaster and thatch, while their Wealden counterparts, perhaps for reasons not entirely unconnected with their traditional craft of iron-smelting, favoured the burnt brick and tile.

Kentish weatherboarding

South-Western Counties

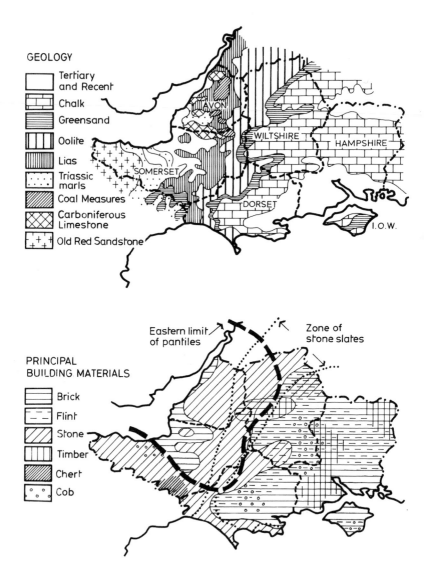

GEOLOGY

- Tertiary and Recent
- Chalk
- Greensand
- Oolite
- Lias
- Triassic marls
- Coal Measures
- Carboniferous Limestone
- Old Red Sandstone

AVON

WILTSHIRE

HAMPSHIRE

SOMERSET

DORSET

I.O.W.

Eastern limit of pantiles

Zone of stone slates

PRINCIPAL BUILDING MATERIALS

- Brick
- Flint
- Stone
- Timber
- Chert
- Cob

3. South-Western Counties

Hampshire, Wiltshire, Dorset, Somerset and Avon

A Region of Thatch and Stone

There is no region of England and Wales so evocative of the remote history of these islands as the counties of the south-west. The open sweeps of chalk uplands with their ancient strongholds, barrows, camps and temples; Bratton and Maiden Castle, Stonehenge, Avebury and Silbury; the Roman remains at Bath, their lead mines on Mendip and the giant Hercules at Cerne Abbas; the legendary and romantic associations of Glastonbury, Athelney and the Somerset levels. These and many features besides lend the region its powerful and sometimes almost brooding sense of the ancient past. It is a region somewhat withdrawn in character.

There is too no area of comparable size in England and Wales that has such a varied geology. In particular, the western counties of Dorset, Somerset and Avon between them provide examples of almost every geological division from the Eocene to the Devonian, a remarkable record for so small an area and one for which the region is famous.

The eastern part of the region, however (broadly, Hampshire, east Dorset and east Wiltshire), shows by contrast a geological consistency and simplicity that is no less striking. It is the country of chalk uplands where most of the prehistoric antiquities survive by reason of the unattractiveness of their thin soils to the farmers of past centuries. The chalklands are bordered on the north-east by the gravelly and sandy heaths lying between Newbury and Aldershot and similarly in the south by the much more extensive area of poor heathy soil stretching from Wareham to Portsmouth and including the whole of the New Forest.

Thus, the region can be roughly divided into two parts: the heathlands and chalk downs of the east, where the buildings are generally of brick, brick and timber or brick and flint, and the complicated and varied hills, valleys and fenlands of the west, where the buildings are generally of stone. But these broad generalisations need elaboration, for there are many different building characteristics within each half of the region and many exceptions to prove the rule. For example, the chalklands produce in addition a mixture of stone, flint and brick, even cob, and in the peat fens of the west and around Bridgwater, although within the half of the region described as generally stoney, the houses are of brick.

Although the walling material of which houses are constructed is of great importance in influencing the building characteristics of the region, it is the roof that has the most profound effect on the appearance of vernacular buildings. Three principal roof types are dominant in the region: thatch in the east and south; stone slates in the north and along the central strip of limestone from Malmesbury to as far south as Bridport; and clay pantiles in the north-west. Each of these roofing materials has its own characteristic shapes, colours and textures, but there is no doubt that it is the thatch that gives this South-western region its special flavour.

To say that thatch follows the chalk in this region, although only approximately true, gives an immediate idea of its general distribution. But in addition, the older traditional cottages of the New Forest are thatched, and in west Dorset and south Somerset thatched buildings extend beyond the chalklands into all the regions south of the Somerset levels. Towards the eastern side of Hampshire, where the character is more akin to that of west Sussex, thatch becomes less universal and tends to give way to plain tiles as a typical roof covering. Here houses are generally of brick or brick and timber in the valleys or brick and flint in the hills. Around Petersfield the chalk is quarried as clunch and forms the walling of many farms, usually built with brick quoins and window and door surrounds, for the chalk is too easily worn away to make satisfactory corners.

All over the eastern part of the region, from the New Forest in the south to the valleys of the chalklands around Salisbury and westwards towards Dorchester and Shaftesbury, the small thatched, one-and-a-half storeyed cottage is the rule. These are

A Wiltshire cottage

what we call 'bun cottages'. Usually steeply pitched at about 55°, their beautifully made roofs give a consistent and homely appearance to the villages. With eyebrows of thatch over the half-dormers and their soft, brown, rounded outlines curving down over their half-hipped ends, the cottages seem more roof than wall, an effect heightened by the technique, logical in a moulded material, of extending the thatch downwards without a break to cover the porch [17]. Unlike the cottages of the South-eastern counties, here the chimneys are placed at one end of the roof, although appearances can be deceptive as many of the cottages were built with outhouse extensions which have been subsequently incorporated into the house proper, resulting in the end chimney now occurring two-thirds of the way along the ridge.

The New Forest region of poor clays and sandy gravels is an area peculiar to itself. Here few very ancient cottages exist. Most are uncompromisingly nineteenth-century in character, built of red brick with plain-tiled roofs and simple Victorian detailing. The few older cottages are traditionally low and whitewashed with thatched roofs and brick chimneys [19].

A New Forest cottage

In exceptionally wealthy places like Beaulieu and Bucklers Hard, where the oak ships of Nelson's time were built, the buildings are richer and generally of red brick with plain-tile roofs: typical products of the eighteenth century. But the predominating characteristic of the traditional cottages of the New Forest region is one of comparative poverty, in sharp contrast to the evident wealth of the region to the west and north in Dorset and Somerset.

Of the many and varied building stones of the region, perhaps the most surprising are the most recent in geological age. The sarsens (or Saracen stones) of the Wiltshire Downs occur as broken up fragments of a layer of hard grey sandstone that lay over the chalk. This layer has been weathered away so that only isolated concentrations of the stones remain, lying like so many sheep upon the grass downs near Marlborough (the stones are also called Grey Wethers, a tribute to their sheep-like appearance). The prehistoric megaliths of Avebury and Stonehenge are made of sarsens. In cottages in the area around Avebury this stone is used in regular squarish blocks and is so hard and difficult to work that little more than a roughly coursed rubble walling is possible. Its cold mauvish-grey imparts a somewhat grim aspect to the houses, ameliorated, it is true, by a good deal of red brickwork, for the stone, though often used in this area of Wiltshire, is by no means universal [23].

Another and less important but no less surprising stone is a coarse sandstone, almost a conglomerate, that borders the chalklands to the south where these give way to the overlying gravels and sands of the southern heaths. The stone, dark chocolate in colour and sometimes called pudding-stone, is used in combination with other paler stones to give a curiously mottled appearance to buildings seen north of Wareham Heath, that broad expanse of undulating, lonely moorland that sets the scene for Thomas Hardy's *The Return of the Native*.

The chalk as usual provides abundant flints, used with brick, cob, clunch and stone. The buildings of the chalklands are characterised by this mixture of materials, an outcome of their scarcity, for all except flint were hard to come by in a landscape that grew few trees, had no clay bottoms and where stone had to be brought from afar [20]. In the wider valleys, soft red brick is common and many fine farms and cottages are built of this pleasant material in combination with thatch [18, 22].

In western Hampshire, all over south Wiltshire and in Dorset, cob has been extensively used in the past and can quite frequently be seen today in roughly plastered and whitewashed cottages nestling beneath their thatch, having the small windows and the slightly rounded, slumped appearance that the material

imparts. Cob (compacted earth or clay used as a walling material)
has been made stronger by the admixture of chalk, but even so its
survival in this area in cottages is not so common as in farmyard
walls and barns, the walls having little thatched roofs to protect
them from the rain.

Mixed materials of the chalklands

From Salisbury westwards, the countryside begins to show in
its buildings the comparative wealth derived from sheep-rearing
and the huge West Country woollen trade. Here the buildings
are mostly constructed of stone in combination with flint and
brick.

Where the western edge of the chalk is broken up by the deep
inroads of the Vales of Pewsey and Wardour, the underlying
Greensand and limestone of the Portland series are uncovered.
The limestone quarries of Chilmark are famous and its village is
well endowed with houses built of the faintly greenish-grey
stone. This stone, together with the Greensand which it closely
resembles in appearance, is not only attractive to pinky-brown
lichens, which give it a welcome warmth of colour, but can also
be cut into smooth rectangular blocks, and this facility gives a
special character to the buildings of the area.

Walling techniques along the Hampshire–Dorset–Wiltshire
borders often include building in chequerboard patterns made
with these square blocks of Greensand or limestone for the lights

Chequer-board walling (near Salisbury)

and knapped flints or brickwork for the darks, a light-hearted device which can be quite roughly handled in cottage walls where irregularity of pattern and occasional inconsistencies in material are acceptable and which also, when accurately built with dressed flints, lends itself to formalised grandeur in larger houses. Further west into Dorset, chequerboard walling is less often seen than horizontal stripes (alternating bands of stones and flints), giving the buildings a no less interesting but more sober appearance.

Banded flint and stone in Dorset

Greensand forms the floor of Pewsey Vale beneath a clayey overlay and makes a continuous strip adjoining the whole length of the chalk escarpments from near Abbotsbury in the south to Swindon in the north. A large area too of south Somerset and west Dorset from Chard to Lyme Regis is on the Greensand. It is a softish grey and brown stone, only sometimes green, and is usually employed squared and evenly coursed, although occasionally ashlared [24].

In the Greensand area of south Somerset an interesting flint-like stone called chert occurs in nodules. It comes in larger pieces than flint and is nearly always yellow-brown in colour, with a not unattractive semi-translucent look. It has been extensively used in the district around Chard in Somerset as a walling material in combination with Greensand stone quoins and is laid in regular courses of small, squarish pieces. In this area, southwards from the Somerset levels to the coast, thatch is the typical roofing material.

West of the Greensand, across the wide valleys formed of the Oxford clay, lies the Oolitic limestone, the stone of the Cotswold hills and of Bath. The band of oolite stretches from the coast near Bridport in a north-north-easterly direction via Bath to the area west of Malmesbury, where the limestone hills are already called the Cotswolds. The same limestone formation continues north-eastwards across England all the way to Scarborough with scarcely a break and forms one of the most consistent features of lowland Britain.

The stone roofing of the limestone belt proper introduces the first notable change in the journey west. Here the buildings are taller and simpler, mostly with long, thin timber lintels over their doors and windows, with simple gabled roofs without parapets, narrow eaves and brick (only occasionally stone) chimneys in the end walls [26]. Older and more opulent houses have stone window mullions supporting stone lintels, covered with a drip-stone (sometimes called a label or hood-mould). Wherever the stone is of better quality and more easily worked, the masonry becomes more regular in squaring, coursing and finishing [21].

Oolitic limestone (by which very generalised classification we mean all Jurassic limestones except the Lias) take many forms and range in colour from the dead white of Portland stone, via the greys of Purbeck to the light browns and honey-greys of the Dorset–Somerset borders and the dark cream of Bath stone. The warm grey stone of the Cotswolds in north Wiltshire is perhaps the best known of all.

At its smoothest the oolite provides the soft brown freestone quarried near Bath on both sides of the Somerset–Wiltshire border. The immediate environs of Bath were heavily developed in the latter parts of the eighteenth and nineteenth centuries, with villas and small middle-class houses built in smooth ashlar which imparts a sort of respectability to their appearance which is curiously difficult to like in spite of the fundamentally beautiful stone.

Further north a combination of brick and stone, poor stuff from the Cornbrash and the Great Oolite, is typical of north-west Wiltshire. Rough stone walls like this are sometimes covered in render or plaster, as can be seen in old houses in such places as Malmesbury and Castle Combe. In this part of the region too, many houses have been colour-washed for so long that their rough walling has built up a protective limey layer of some thickness.

Colour-washed rough stone (Malmesbury, Wiltshire)

The stone slates of the limestone regions lend their buildings a totally different character to that of the cosier thatched buildings to the east, a character at once more harmonious and more severe. The slates take subtly different forms according to the local characteristics of the material.

In the north of the region, the Cotswold limestones make for small slates, needing fairly steep pitches of 45° to 50° [26]. These slates are rough-textured and were traditionally made by watering the quarried or mined stones and allowing the winter frosts to split them into thin slabs. The slates are carefully graded in size from large at the eaves to very small stones, no more than four inches (100 mm) across, at the ridge, the general impression being one of a sophisticated craftsmanship serving a wealthy community.

Purbeck stone roofs

In the extreme south, by contrast, notably at Swanage and Corfe Castle and in the Purbeck Hills, large slabs of Purbeck limestone can be got; these can be laid at low pitches and are extremely heavy. Here the stones are often laid in mortar to keep out the driving rain from the sea, giving the roof a smudged-over appearance that goes rather well with the modest size of the cottages, which are made to seem even smaller by the scale of their roofing slabs [27]. Dormers or secondary gables, with valleys between the intersecting roof shapes which can be 'swept' with the smaller stones, are a persistant feature of the northern part of the limestone belt; but with the larger and clumsier stones from the extreme south, simpler roof forms are required and, although a good many dormers are still seen, these are crudely achieved and the general effect is far more primitive.

All stone tiles produce, as do pantiles, clear-cut geometric shapes for the roofs. This lends the stone-roofed areas a classical quality which is heightened by their homogeneity, roofs, walls and, frequently in the older and wealthier houses, window mullions too being formed from the same material. It is this unity of the limestone belt cottages and houses that gives rise to the appearance of having 'grown out of the ground' that is so often attributed to them.

Beyond and beneath the oolite, with its flat-topped, rather dull uplands, the Liassic limestones emerge. These create a more broken and interesting landscape. The stone is of various colours, blue, white and yellow Lias being the most important and noticeable. From Lyme Regis for some distance inland, in the middle of the region around Somerton and forming islands in the Somerset marshes, the blue Lias lends its cool (some say gloomy) grey to the buildings [25]. This stone is found in shallow layers, between deep bands of soft clayey shale. The stone layers

Thin stones from the Lias (Somerset)

are so regular that they can be used for walling without other thicknessing and impart a curiously mean and even appearance to the buildings which is unmistakable; moreover, the mortar with which the buildings are put together is often darker than the stone, which does little to soften this impression [28].

Yellow Lias is one of the most famous of the many building stones of the region. It is quarried at Hamden Hill in Somerset and is known as Ham Hill stone. It is a pretty, dark brownish-yellow, sandy limestone, made even more agreeable by its attraction for pale grey lichens, and is used in the neighbourhood of Montacute. The stone is readily sawn and shaped and makes ideal dressings for windows and door jambs. Further away from its source, it can be seen used in this manner in combination with blue Lias walling—but the contrast between the blue and the orangey-brown is rather too sharp to be pleasant.

Throughout all lowland areas in the region adjoining the Bristol Channel, most buildings are roofed in pantiles, although these are far more extensively used in the East of England (see Chapters 5 and 8). Pantiles come in many shapes, but the most usual are the flat-and-roll, the S-curved and the true Bridgwater tile: the flat-and-two-rolls.

Pantiles were brought from abroad in the seventeenth century into Bridgwater and distributed from there up the Bristol Channel and, more importantly for our region, up the Avon, the Parrett and the Yeo to the interior of Somerset and west Wiltshire as far as the Vale of Pewsey. By the eighteenth century pantiles were being made in Bridgwater which then became the centre for their production in the West of England. Their distribution extended no further than the inland waterways would permit, so the boundaries of their influence are quite sharply defined. In combination with stone or brick, they give the buildings a precise formal appearance totally at variance with the soft and indeterminate character of thatch [25].

Because of their size and brittle nature pantiles only lend themselves to very simple roof shapes; it is difficult to cut them diagonally to make a hip or valley, so gabled roofs are the rule, dormers and hips virtually unknown. Therefore pantiled buildings are nearly always of two storeys, in contrast to the generality of the thatched cottages of the chalklands, which are more often of one-and-a-half storeys. Practically all stone buildings with pantiled roofs, other than very humble cottages, have parapets to their gables. The tiles are generally brown or a cheerful subdued red, which makes an entirely satisfactory combination with grey stone. Pantiles can be laid to pitches as low as 30° without letting in the water, but here in the West Country they are almost invariably laid on much steeper roofs (up to 55°), not only where pantiles were used to replace thatch but seemingly in many cases built to that pitch originally. This is probably because traditional building methods die hard and in surrounding areas buildings commonly have the more steeply pitched roofs of stone tiles and thatch, materials that were universal before the arrival of the pantile.

Simple roof shapes in pantiles (Somerset)

The brick houses around Bridgwater, with their steep pantiled roofs, seen in association with the muddy tidal waterways of the district, are strongly reminiscent of the Netherlands, in spite of the fact that most of the trade out of Bridgwater was with the Biscay and Spanish ports. The pantiles themselves were however imported from Holland or Belgium, partly in exchange for wool and woollen cloth. Somerset and the neighbouring counties produced excellent West of England broadcloth, which was in great demand all over Europe, and although the cloth trade in this part of England declined in the seventeenth century, Bridgwater was a major centre in the West Country for overseas trade. Here no Dutch gables are in evidence like those in East Anglia; gable parapets are straight (and in humbler cottages absent); chimneys are placed at the ends of the houses; windows and door-heads are nearly always of segmental brick arches. The bricks are red and the streets of this area look as different as can be from those of the remainder of the region.

West beyond Bridgwater, the Quantock Hills, the Brendon Hills and Exmoor itself are composed of warm grey hard stone from the ancient Devonian series. The villages surrounding the hills however are mostly built of the red and pink stones from the New Red Sandstones of the valleys.

Like the hills of the west, the Mendips produce a hard, intractable stone (this time from the Carboniferous Limestone), whose use for building is not widespread. It is mauvish-grey, sometimes with red streaks in it, and lends a distinct lavender shade to the few rough buildings of the area.

The Mendips are generally sparsely populated with isolated farmhouses. Cottages, as is so often the case in ancient mining or quarrying districts, are more frequently seen in rows than singly. Roofs are again nearly all pantiled, and the dark grey of the stonework is sometimes covered with welcome whitewash which makes a brave attempt to relieve the desolate and almost sinister air that permeates the landscape, scarred by worked-out lead mines and peopled by the ghosts of an industry long since departed.

17

18

19

20

SOUTH-WESTERN COUNTIES

17 Tidpit, HAMPSHIRE. Brick and stone combined, with thatch swept down over the porch (*page 37*)

18 Chilton Foliat, WILTSHIRE. Warm red brick and thatch, typical of the Kennet valley (*page 39*)

19 Godshill, HAMPSHIRE. A small New Forest cottage, probably made of cob (*page 38*)

20 Hurstbourne Tarrant, HAMPSHIRE. A typical brick and flint cottage of the chalklands (*page 39*)

21

22

23

24

SOUTH-WESTERN COUNTIES

21 Marnhull, DORSET. A fine limestone house in a quarrying village (*page 42*)

22 Tidpit, HAMPSHIRE. A well built farmhouse (*page 39*)

23 East Kennet, near Marlborough, WILTSHIRE. Cold grey sarsen stones combined with red brick (*page 39*)

24 Donhead St Mary, WILTSHIRE. Large blocks of greensand give quality to this small cottage (*page 42*)

25

26

27

28

SOUTH-WESTERN COUNTIES

25 Shapwick, SOMERSET. Blue Lias stone and pantiles in the Polden Hills (*pages 45 & 46*)

26 Charlton, WILTSHIRE. A stone-built house bordering the Cotswolds, with rubble walls and oak lintels (*pages 42 & 44*)

27 Worth Matravers, DORSET. Stone cottages in the heart of the Purbeck quarrying region (*page 44*)

28 Somerton, SOMERSET. Cottages built with thin blue Lias stones (*page 46*)

29

30

31

32

DEVON AND CORNWALL

29 Northlew, DEVON. Whitewash and thatch in the Culm Measures (*page 56*)
30 Dittisham, DEVON. Whitewashed stone cottage with typical tapered stone chimney (*page 63*)
31 Farmhouse near Sidmouth, DEVON. Tall side chimney and thatch (*page 56*)
32 Atherington, DEVON. Thatched cottage with cob walls built against the stone chimney (*pages 51 & 58*)

There is a simple pattern in the varied vernacular buildings of this region: 'bun' cottages in the east, two-storeyed stone houses in the west, and thatch throughout all districts except for the pantiled area of the north-west and the stone tile belt in the centre.

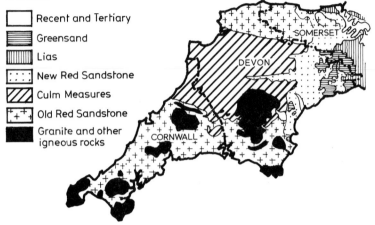

GEOLOGY

- Recent and Tertiary
- Greensand
- Lias
- New Red Sandstone
- Culm Measures
- Old Red Sandstone
- Granite and other igneous rocks

SOMERSET
DEVON
CORNWALL

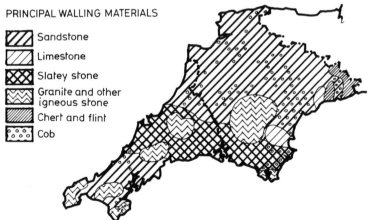

PRINCIPAL WALLING MATERIALS

- Sandstone
- Limestone
- Slatey stone
- Granite and other igneous stone
- Chert and flint
- Cob

Devon and Cornwall

4. Devon and Cornwall

Thatch and Cob, Slate and Granite

Devon and Cornwall, forming as they do the south-west peninsula of Britain, somewhat isolated from the remainder of England by moors and rivers, form together a recognisable geographical area. The rugged coastline, the terrifying cliffs of the north, the long, winding, drowned valleys of the south, the bare granite moorlands and the minute, crowded harbours are all common to both counties and help to reinforce the single Devon-and-Cornwall concept in the mind.

In fact however much of the apparent similarity between the two counties proves to be misleading, for Devon and Cornwall are in very many respects totally dissimilar. Where Devon is soft, Cornwall is hard; where the former is essentially rural, much of the Cornish landscape is industrial; where the typical Cornish house is precise, low-pitched, slate-roofed and built of blocks of grey-brown granite [33], Devonshire houses are more generously proportioned, taller, for the most part thatched, steep-pitched and built of red rubble-stone or of white-washed cob [32]. Few people who lose their hearts to Devon find Cornwall sympathetic, while enthusiasts for the more astringent Cornish scene think Devon too pretty and bland.

The romantic and historical associations of the counties are also of very different characters. Devon is inevitably linked in the minds of all Englishmen with the Armada, with Sir Francis Drake and the exploits of the Elizabethan seamen. Cornwall by contrast seems a more mysterious land, drawing its magic from a remoter past. Although both counties were inhabited by the peoples whose stone circles, menhirs and cromlechs (called quoits in Cornwall) still stand on the granite hills and headlands,

Cornwall is also steeped in legends whose origins lie in the Dark Ages, legends of the Pendragon, King Arthur, the romance of Avalon and the lost land of Lyonesse. Phoenicians traded in Cornish creeks for tin before the Roman conquest, while in more recent centuries the county's many small harbours, coves and inlets, and its close affinities with Brittany, have provided opportunities for smuggling, for long the subject of romantic fiction.

Geologically the region is dominated by the huge granite bosses of Dartmoor and Bodmin Moor and the smaller but still very large granite masses further west which culminate in the Land's End peninsula itself. It is these resistant granite and other igneous masses that give the area its highly distinctive physical character, accounting not only for the deeply indented coastline and high moorlands, but for the presence around their edges of the rocks and minerals that have been mined, quarried or streamed from the rivers from time immemorial. Around the periphery of the granite and lava masses, tin and copper have been concentrated in veins, the surrounding shales and clays have been baked and compressed into slate, and the weathering and consequent breakdown of the granite into fine clay has given rise to the china clay industry whose high white pyramids of spoil cover a huge area of Hensbarrow Downs behind St Austell, making in their gleaming purity a strange contrast with the black tips of the coalmining areas elsewhere in England and Wales.

The igneous rocks themselves, although hard and difficult to work, have been used for building from the Iron Age and include, beside the all-important granite, such exotically named but minor building stones as porphyry from the south, serpentine from the Lizard, and elvan, polyphant and catacleuse occurring locally in the north and east of Cornwall. Until quite recently granite was too hard to quarry and most buildings were made of moor-stones—blocks of granite picked up from the surface of the land or found in the clitter of rocks, weathered out from the tors which themselves break up into nearly rectangular lumps. Consequently the older granite buildings are made of stones of all sizes, ranging from gigantic boulders forming the lowest part of the house wall, and huge roughly dressed corner-stones, to smaller, irregularly squared pieces in the rubble walling. Some of the boulders are so large that it is virtually certain that the house was built against the stone rather than that the stone was brought to the house-place. Later buildings are made from quarried rock, cut to required sizes and laid with regular joints in proper courses, which gives them a less romantic appearance. Granite is a noble rock, massive, hard, durable and coarse-grained. In this region it is light in tone, varying in colour from pale grey, via pale buff, to quite a full rusty brown, and the character it imparts to the buildings is a notable aspect of the vernacular style of the area.

Granite farmhouse (Cornwall)

Apart from granite, the peninsula is nearly all made of sandstones, shales and slates through which the granite masses protrude. South-west of a line from Tintagel in the north to Torquay in the south, the whole area is composed of rocks from the Old Red Sandstone and this formation also makes the massive bulk of Exmoor. Between lies a very large region comprising the Culm Measures (shales, sandstones and clays, all of the Carboniferous period), which form a rather monotonous, rolling upland landscape giving rise to no very rich farming land and providing few building materials. The lack of good timber for building in the region has meant that there are few timber buildings in Devon and none in Cornwall. The abundant clays however, taken together with a lack of fuel for brick-making, have given rise to the widespread use of cob for walling wherever building stone could not be more easily got.

Cob is made of compacted clay and earth, bound with straw and moulded in various ways to form thick walls finished with lime plaster. It must be kept dry, so cob houses are always built on a stone or brick plinth. When the plaster comes off, the cob deteriorates very quickly.

North of Bodmin Moor and to a lesser extent south-west of Dartmoor all the way to Fowey, the shales and clays have been changed to slate and slatey rocks. The principal slate quarry for the whole region is at Delabole, north-west of Bodmin Moor, a spectacular pit in the ground over four hundred feet deep and a third of a mile across, producing pale and dark-grey slates that are used for roofing and slate-hanging for many miles around as well as being exported, originally from little harbours like Port Isaac on the north coast, to all over the South of England and across the water to South Wales.

In the east of Devon, east of Exeter and Tiverton, there is a broad band of New Red Sandstone. This is the heartland of Devon, where the earth is a bright, dark pinky-red (a truly startling colour, much stronger than elsewhere in Britain), the fields are brilliant green and the dairy farms are large and prosperous. This is the area which evokes everyone's image of Devon: rich, cosy and a little lush.

East of this part of Devon again, in the extreme corner of the county, is a small area north of Sidmouth and Lyme Regis where the tumbled hills of Greensand and the Lias spread over the border from Dorset. Here there is no great difference in the building style from that of the neighbouring county; the principal building materials are cob and thatch with some chalkstone and flint and a good deal of horny-looking chert, that pale-brown variety of flint from the Greensand. At Beer, a whitish shelly limestone is quarried from the Chalk; called Beerstone, it is much harder than ordinary chalkstone and can be seen in many buildings in the district, used in squarish blocks in combination with flint and chert.

Flint, chert and Beerstone (Devon)

West of Sidmouth, the Devon style of building begins to assert itself. Here, south and east of Exeter, the land supports rich farms and the farmhouses all have very tall side chimneys, standing up like stalks above the eaves beside the entrance doorways. Farm after farm is built to this pattern. The chimneys are always built of grey and red stone up as far as the eaves and sometimes above as well, but more usually the tall upper and narrower part of the stack is built in brick, often with a slate lid on the top supported on corner bricks. The chimneys are broad at the base, stepping inwards with sloping slated shoulders two or three times before reaching just above the eaves level, where the tall thin stack takes off. In older stone examples, the stack is thicker and often irregularly shaped.

Devonshire side chimney

The houses themselves are usually built of rich, dark cocoa-coloured cob, which is colour-washed in pale buffs and creams.

Roofs are thatched and the angle between the tall chimney and the sloping roof behind, where water would otherwise lodge and find an entry, is bridged with a small subsidiary roof of its own [31]. In a village like Otterton, near Budleigh Salterton, the scene is made by the forest of tall side chimneys all along the street of colour-washed and thatched cob houses, resting on black painted flint bases.

Side chimneys like these occur sporadically throughout Devon and are once again a notable feature in the north of the county. Around Bideford and across Exmoor to Porlock and beyond, the pattern is similar: thatched houses of colour-washed stone or cob with tall stalked side chimneys. The curious occurrence of side chimneys beside the main entrance porch in certain large and antique farmhouses in north Pembrokeshire is an interesting parallel. A few north Devon chimneys are round, and those in north Pembrokeshire, although shorter, are almost universally so. There does seem to be some affinity between the two areas in these respects and certainly there was trade in wool across the water between the West of England and 'Little England beyond Wales'. In fact it is recorded that commerce between St David's and Barnstaple was common in the seventeenth century. The very ancient and primitive-looking hall house at Tintagel, now the Post Office, also has a massive side chimney.

The thatch in much of Devon is less opulent-looking than that of adjoining Dorset; the eaves are if anything shallower and the thatch itself looks thinner and straighter [29]. Certainly the curved and plastic treatment of thatch that is such a feature of Hampshire and east Dorset is absent in these larger Devonshire buildings.

South of Dartmoor lies the projecting triangle of land between Torquay and Plymouth containing the area of the South Hams. Many ridges of dolerites and lavas and a few areas of pink and grey Devonian limestone, hard enough in some cases to be classed as a marble, occur in the district, where there is a good deal of slate and slatey stone as well. Around Totnes and in the town itself, hung slates are used as a protection against the weather. The pale, silvery-grey, sometimes blue-grey slates can be seen in many houses in the area, and thatch, although not infrequent on the smaller and more rural houses, is no longer universal. Chimneys in this district are conventionally located at the ends of the buildings and are thick and squat, slightly tapered above slate watershed courses.

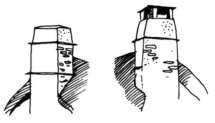

Chimneys in the South Hams (Devon)

The high mass of Dartmoor, although open and deserted on the bare tops, has many sheltered valleys along its flanks. Quite high up the valleys there are fine old farmhouses built of granite, with long thatched roofs covering house, byre and barn. The latter are often built downhill from the house and the whole roof ridge dips down over the outhouses following the slope of the ground in a manner not seen elsewhere. (Similar farmhouses in Cumbria or the Pennines are more often built parallel to the contours with a level ridge.) The sloping roof ridge gives the Dartmoor farmhouse an indeterminacy of outline that merges it with the landscape in a manner curiously at variance with its sturdy granite walling. The older farms in the area date from the early seventeenth century, their granite walls showing grey-

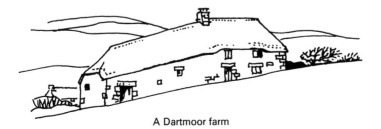

A Dartmoor farm

brown, made with huge blocks of stone. In the grander houses, the windows have stone mullions and there is occasionally some decorative feature over door or porch. Decoration in hard, coarse-grained granite is always crude and simple since it can only be carved in low relief. In humbler buildings, lintels over doors and windows are long, rectangular blocks of granite.

North of Dartmoor stretches the extensive area of the Culm Measures. Here as elsewhere in so much of Devonshire the older houses, mostly in the villages, are colour-washed or whitewashed and are built of cob or shaley stone or a combination of the two. Stone is used for chimneys, and where these occur in end walls the cob is built up around the masonry to complete the wall [32]. Stone is occasionally used for the ground storey, with a cob first floor above.

First-floor rooms are never in the roof space in Devonshire houses, which are virtually all of two full storeys, the roof shape being simple, with either a full hip, a half-hip or a plain gable.

Side chimneys occur occasionally throughout the region of the Culm in the older houses but they are by no means a general feature. Many nineteenth-century buildings in this area are roofed in slate and may conceal, behind their precise and rather unsympathetic whitewashed exteriors, walls built of cob like those of their predecessors.

Exmoor itself, being made of sandstone, supports a good deal of farming land quite high up. It was cleared of forest comparatively recently, so most of the large farms are eighteenth-century and rather grand. The landscape too in the cultivated parts expresses, with its straight beech hedges and well organised look, its comparatively late emergence as habitable farmland.

The Tamar marks the boundary between Devonshire and Cornwall and seldom does a county boundary follow so logical a course with such consistency. Once across the river, the character of the country and its buildings seems to change. Place names sprout a typically Cornish list of unheard of and unlikely saints and names such as Menheniot, Trevigro and Pensilva proclaim that a frontier has been crossed.

In the gap between the granite bosses of Dartmoor and

Bodmin Moor are many minor outcrops of granite and lava. Where the Tamar cuts through these, in a steeply winding wooded gorge, Devon Great Consuls and the Consolidated Cornish Copper Mines flourished in their short period of intense activity in the nineteenth century, when for little more than fifty years they were together the largest producers of copper in the world. Nineteenth-century miners' terraces, slate-roofed and built of brown stone, are a feature of the area, which is otherwise dominated by the ruined engine houses and lonely chimneys marking where the beam engines pumped the mines.

A Cornish fishing village

Fishing villages such as Polperro and others round the coasts of Cornwall are famous for the minute, steeply twisting alleyways between the whitewashed stone and cob houses which crowd down to the sea in whatever room is available in the narrow coves of the cliff-bound coast. The intricacy of the layout of such places gives some credence to their claim to have been able to hide contraband from the excise-men. Roofs in the fishing villages are of slate, and most buildings are protected from the storms by a coat of render or by hung slates. All buildings are colour-washed or whitewashed, and many slate roofs and even some hung slates are slurried over with mortar to keep out the driving damp.

Above St Austell, among the china clay workings of Hensbarrow Downs (these uncompromising granite moorlands are called 'downs' in Cornwall, which seems singularly inappropriate to anyone brought up in Wiltshire or Sussex), alongside the general industrial mess, old quarrymen's cottages can be found, beautifully built of closely jointed and squared granite blocks, slate-roofed and perfect [34].

Around Camborne and Redruth is an industrial area where modern tin-mining is carried on, and here it is difficult to find among the activity any very distinctive character in the buildings. Granite and slate are the rule, and the old mine chimneys brood over the scene, standing sentinel all around the built-up areas on the hillsides. The mine chimneys are all of a pattern: standing beside the tall-gabled and roofless engine-houses, arched openings gaping emptily to the sky, the circular chimneys are built of stone for two-thirds of their considerable height and thereafter finished in brick (usually blue but occasionally red), presumably because the taper on the chimney made the radius inconveniently small at that point for building in stone.

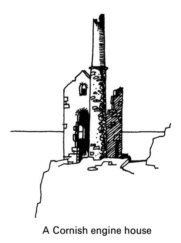

A Cornish engine house

South of the Camborne area lies the Lizard peninsula, made mostly of dark-green and red-veined serpentine rock, centring on a high, flat moorland called Goonhilly Down where the Post Office has its transmission and receiving station. Strangely enough, there is a tradition of thatched roofs here: the only part of Cornwall we have found where any considerable area is consistently thatched. The warm thatch comes as a change from the universal slate. The village of Cadgwith on the south-east coast tumbles down its little valley and up the other side in a tide of brown, furry roofs that must be remarkably well secured to withstand the gales of such an exposed coast. Most cottages in the area are whitewashed and are built of stone, or, in many cases, with stone for their lower floors and cob above. Occasionally eighteenth- and nineteenth-century cottages can be seen built of unwhitewashed blocks of serpentine whose exotic dark green makes an interesting building material [35]. Although it has a reputation for unreliability, and so is seldom used in large or important buildings, serpentine has nevertheless some significance for the vernacular buildings in this limited area.

The Land's End peninsula, being entirely composed of granite, is a unique area combining many virtues. An open, deep-Atlantic rock-bound coast; the romance of ancient, deserted mines, their beam engines standing no more than thirty feet above the waves or perched perilously above the fabulous cliffs; a comparatively wealthy farming community that has left a legacy of fine farmhouses, all built of massive granite blocks; and magnificent megalithic quoits and standing stones.

Roofs in this extremely exposed region are understandably all slurried over with mortar or, less often, tarred to keep them on and to make them as watertight as possible [33]. The technique, common in Pembrokeshire, of stretching wires over the roof from eaves to eaves and cementing them in with mortar to form ridges running down the roof four or five feet apart, is sometimes seen in west Cornwall. The affinity of this area with south-west Wales, visually and in feeling, is very marked.

Only the very grand farms and manor houses, of which there are extremely few, have parapetted gables. One farm in the area has kneelers made in the form of rounded granite projections decorated with roughly incised spirals or volutes. A precisely similar detail is to be seen in Blisland, on Bodmin, a long way inland, executed almost certainly by the same mason. The liking

An unusual carved kneeler (near Blisland)

for rounded decoration is consistent with the egg-shaped granite boulders from the beach, which are used on Land's End farms for decorating their gateposts and as bollards at farmyard entrances, sometimes whitewashed and sometimes painted shiny black.

A Land's End farm

Because of their airy, cliff-top situation, the long terraces of miners' cottages, stone-built and slate-roofed, at St Just and other coastal mining communities seem less grim than their industrial counterparts elsewhere. The more prosperous of these little nineteenth-century cottages have fine glazed porches, a great feature of Cornish houses of a certain date and size [35].

These are often elaborately designed, nearly always with highly coloured glass panes (red, blue, green and yellow), and are always filled to overflowing with flowering plants, usually geraniums, which press their petals against the coloured glass and form exotic little oases in their rather bleak, wet granite and slate surroundings.

Cornish coloured glass porches

The older houses in this part of Cornwall are massively built of bare granite rubble. Windows are small, unless, as is usually the case, they have been enlarged to take the almost universal squarish eighteenth- and nineteenth-century sashes. Chimneys are broad and squat, with no protection at the top such as is seen in Devon or Cumbria [30]. Often the top course of stones around the chimney is stepped back above a slightly projecting slate course, which gives the Cornish domestic roof an unmistakable profile.

Further north, around Delabole and its slate mine, the scene changes again. Slate rock, thin and hard, is used for buildings: slate lintels or shallow arches made with slates over the doors and windows, slate garden paths, hung slate on the walls—even the porches are made of huge, thin slabs of slate, one up either side and one across the top, or with two sloping slates to make a pitched roof [36].

Devon and Cornwall, although different in the character of their buildings and of their countryside, have many common attributes, not least (from our point of view) that of an almost total absence of timber buildings of any sort. There is no doubt that the main characteristics of the region are due to three basic but very different materials: cob, slate and granite.

33

34

35

36

DEVON AND CORNWALL

33 Near Zennor, Lands End, CORNWALL. Granite farmhouse with a slurried slate roof (*pages 51 & 61*)

34 Near St Austell, CORNWALL. Granite quarryman's cottage among the clay tips (*page 60*)

35 Kuggar, Lizard, CORNWALL. Dark green blocks of serpentine (*pages 61 & 62*)

36 Delabole, CORNWALL. Hung-slate walls; roof, chimney and porch all of slate from the quarry (*page 63*)

EAST ANGLIA

37 Hunstanton, NORFOLK. A mixture of clunch, flint, carstone and brick (*pages 71 & 72*)
38 Worstead, NORFOLK. Brick and pantiled cottages (*page 73*)
39 Binham, NORFOLK. Bright-red pantiles contrast with pale flint cobbles (*pages 70 & 72*)
40 Much Hadham, HERTFORDSHIRE. This house is weatherboarded in the East Anglian tradition (*page 78*)

41

42

43

44

EAST ANGLIA

41 Kersey, SUFFOLK. Gabled timber-framed houses in a rich Suffolk village (*page 76*)
42 Monks Eleigh, SUFFOLK. Thatch and plaster cottages (*page 77*)
43 Clare, SUFFOLK. Early pargetting on a jettied house (*pages 75 & 76*)
44 Stoke-by-Nayland, SUFFOLK. A consistent tradition in plaster and colour-wash (*page 76*)

45

46

47

48

EAST ANGLIA

45 Near Great Sampford, ESSEX. Long straight roof shape, typical of Cambridge and Essex (*page 78*)

46 Fenstanton, CAMBRIDGESHIRE. Low brick cottages with brindled tiled roofs (*pages 74 & 78*)

47 Haslingfield, CAMBRIDGESHIRE. Cottage with pentice boards to protect the plaster on the gable wall (*page 77*)

48 Great Bardfield, ESSEX. An old plastered farmhouse with central chimney (*page 74*)

5. East Anglia and the Southern Fens

Norfolk, Suffolk, Essex and Cambridgeshire

Colour-washed Plaster, Brick and Flint

East Anglia is an almost stoneless region of recent geological age and is virtually flat, the land nowhere rising to a height of much more than four hundred feet. In spite of these apparently unpromising characteristics it is a region of very great interest, variety and individuality.

The region divides into three recognisably different areas: the fenlands of the west, the chalklands and heathlands of the north, east and centre, and the rich valley lands of the south and east.

The chalklands and fens are austere regions of high winds and big skies, while the rolling valley country of the south-east is soft and intimate, with its treed and winding valleys, its meadows and full streams. This is the Constable country, while the heathlands of the north-east are associated more with the wilder, uncultivated scenery so often painted by the Norwich School.

The building types of the area can in the same way be broadly grouped in three categories: the brick buildings of the fenlands and heathlands, the rather uncompromising flint buildings of the Chalk, and the generally more opulent-seeming and antique timber buildings of the heavily wooded valley country, glowing with all the buffs, yellows and apricot shades of colour-washed plaster. Within these main categories of building types there is considerable variety, brought about to a large extent by the blanket of superficial glacial deposits that cover so much of the area and conceal its basically simple underlying structure.

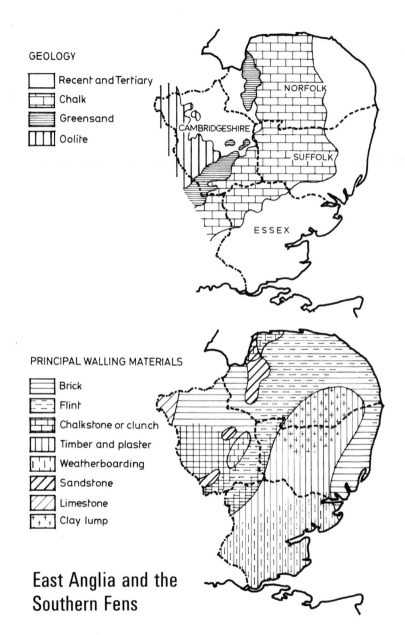

GEOLOGY

- ☐ Recent and Tertiary
- ▦ Chalk
- ▤ Greensand
- ▥ Oolite

NORFOLK

CAMBRIDGESHIRE

SUFFOLK

ESSEX

PRINCIPAL WALLING MATERIALS

- ☰ Brick
- ┅ Flint
- ▦ Chalkstone or clunch
- ▥ Timber and plaster
- ▤ Weatherboarding
- ▨ Sandstone
- ◪ Limestone
- ⁺⁺⁺ Clay lump

East Anglia and the Southern Fens

Although for much of its history East Anglia has had close contact with Flanders and the Netherlands, it has been to a large extend isolated from the rest of England and this has been an important factor in developing the individual character of the region. The impenetrable forests of the south-eastern claylands and the equally impassable western fens left only a narrow upland chalk highway in between to the rest of England, and although in time the forests were cleared and the fens were drained, this was not before isolation had had its effect on regional character.

In early medieval times East Anglia was highly populated; in fact, by the eleventh century Norfolk was the most densely populated county in England. Later, its sheep farming and wool trade had made it one of the wealthiest too, and, as in many other parts of England, the fifteenth century saw the building of a great many huge and splendid parish churches financed by wool.

Because of its close contact with the Continent, East Anglia was the first region to import bricks into England and to set up brickyards for local manufacture. It was not until the seventeenth century however that bricks were used in any quantity for small houses, the few earlier ones being sometimes built of Flemish bricks brought into the country in the returning wool boats.

Flemish weavers had been encouraged to settle in England since medieval times, when Edward III invited them over to develop the weaving trade. Flemish influence on building styles can be seen in the ports and small towns where the Flemish immigrants mostly settled, but also inland villages in the east of the region have houses with crow-stepped gables and, in later examples, curved 'Dutch' gables, both of Flemish origin.

Crow-stepped and Dutch gables

East Anglia, being on the whole rather flat, lacks much water power, and when in the seventeenth century more powerful machinery was needed for cloth manufacture (due to improved techniques, which included 'fulling') the industry in the region began to decline, for the weavers then favoured the limestone hills with their faster streams, such as the Stroud Valley in the Cotswolds and the Avon Valley near Bradford-on-Avon. So by the eighteenth century East Anglia's wool prosperity had declined, and its still relatively isolated situation enabled it to escape much nineteenth-century development, leaving us, as the legacy of its boom years, its fine timbered buildings.

The history of the fenlands is long and sporadic. The Romans drained the silt fens bordering the Wash, but it was not until the seventeenth century that any very successful attempt was made to drain the peat fens round Cambridge, Huntingdon and Ely. Dutch engineers were engaged for the task; they were extremely unpopular with the local people because draining the fens threatened their traditional fenny way of life. The silt which forms the northern fens and the beds of all the streams is a fairly stable material, but peat shrinks enormously when dried, which is why the southern fens lie so far below their streams, which now stand on embankments of their own silt. First wind-pumps, and then, as the height that the water had to be pumped increased with the shrinking fen, steam engines were used for drainage. Today, the remains of the wind-pumps (circular towers of brick, like small windmills) and the big Victorian engine-houses can be seen in many parts of the fenland.

The fen islands and the margins of the fen have been occupied for many centuries, but these areas seem never to have experienced periods of any great wealth. Buildings in the area are consequently modest, although some are of considerable age. Most are of brick, for the area was completely cleared of woodland by the sixteenth century. The fens themselves, those strange, geometrical landscapes, are sparsely populated with small, well spaced farmhouses, nearly all of Victorian date.

Brick clays occur in very many localities in East Anglia, to the extent that brick buildings can be found virtually everywhere.

Perhaps the most important of the brick clays is the Gault, which underlies the Chalk and outcrops in the west of the region, giving rise to the pale yellow (usually called 'white') bricks of Cambridgeshire and west Norfolk. Many other East Anglian brick clays produce pale bricks due to the lack of iron in the clay. To the east of the region some brick clays bake to a strong reddish-brown which gives a warmer and more positive character to the buildings. But there is no doubt that, although brick buildings can be found almost anywhere in the region and do in fact predominate in the fens and in the north-east, the principal materials of the valley country are timber and plaster and that of the chalklands is flint.

The chalklands of Norfolk, with their layer of boulder clay, provide nothing better to build with than rough flints from the surface of the land. In the Breckland area of west Norfolk and north-west Suffolk the overlying sands give rise to heathlands and pinewoods, but from prehistoric times flints have been quarried and mined from the underlying chalk for tools, weapons and, later, for building materials. There is still a local industry for cutting and shaping flints round Brandon in the Breckland, whose origins reach back into prehistory. Here the flints are opened to expose the dark, slatey grey of their interior and then squared: a technique called 'knapping' that is most effective

Pebble built cottage of north Norfolk

when used to make the carefully formed and neat infill to stone walling in grand buildings like the huge fifteenth-century wool churches. But in the Breckland the humbler buildings are made with halved flints, built quite roughly, uncoursed and un-squared, with the broken dark side showing.

In north and east Norfolk the houses are built with cobbles—that is, of rough unbroken flints from the fields, showing their knobbly, whitish exterior coating, laid, as with the Breckland flints, random and not coursed [39]. Along the coast, flint pebbles from the beach are used, and these, being of a more uniform shape than the cobbles, are often laid in neat courses, are generally smaller in scale and are, moreover frequently white-washed or tarred on faces exposed to the weather.

Brick and flint (Norfolk)

All flint cottages (we have found only one exception in England) have brick or stone corners and surrounds to doors and windows, with shallow segmental brick arches above, because to form corners and arches with round or knobbly flints is not really practical. Bricks in the Breckland and in the surrounding regions are pale yellow, and the combination of the slaty grey of split flints and the pale yellow of the bricks is a most characteristic feature of these buildings, lending the towns and villages of the area a pale, aloof, some would say cold character, in strong contrast to the comparative cosiness of the valley country.

Roofs in these areas are almost invariably covered in pantiles. The older houses, where the pantiles have replaced earlier thatch, have their roofs at what seems an unnecessarily steep pitch, usually 50° to 55°. This imparts a strong emphasis to the roof that is most pleasing and characteristic. More recent buildings that were roofed in pantiles from the outset have a more normal pitch of about 40°. Roofs in this area are gabled. Hips and half-hips are uncharacteristic, because pantiles are difficult to cut and hipped roofs require the tiles to be cut diagonally.

Pantiled dormers (Norfolk)

Typically, buildings are of one-and-a-half storeys—that is to say, the upper storey is smaller because it is in the roof, lit with dormer windows. Dormers are roofed with pantiles, their roofs running with the slope of the main roof but at a gentler angle, a device that makes for a harmonious design and seems the direct outcome of the logical use of an intractable roofing material [37]. Chimneys are located on the gable ends of the cottages (not generally in the centre of the roof, as in the timber houses further south in the region).

More particularly in the older buildings, gable walls are taken above the tiles to form low, sloping parapets. Where thick thatch has been replaced by much thinner pantiles, the parapets of

course look absurdly high and ungainly. It is in the embellish-
ment of the gable parapets with crow-steps or curved brickwork,
reminiscent of Dutch town houses, that the Continental
influence can best be seen. Window and door frames in the flint
buildings are placed forward, flush with the face of the brick
jambs, not recessed as might be expected [39]. The reason for
this is obscure, for although such an arrangement makes for a
nice deep window sill inside, it affords no weather protection to
the frame and makes it difficult to keep out driving rain.

Thus, the scene in the chalklands is one of grey and yellow
walls, occasionally tarred or whitewashed near the coast, and
steep, brownish-red pantiled roofs, gabled, with narrow eaves
and with dormer windows roofed in sloping pantiles like the
houses.

Towards the north-west of Norfolk, north of Downham
Market, the chalk forms a considerable scarp, beneath which the
Greensand is exposed. Round Hunstanton the lower Chalk
(where the rock is hard enough to use as a building stone, called
clunch) is stained a bright Indian red and the underlying
Greensand is a dark reddish chocolate colour. The sequence of
colour in the rocks (white–pink–red–chocolate) can be perfectly
seen at the foot of the cliffs from the beach at Hunstanton. The
astonishing variety of building materials used in this north-west
corner of the county is a measure of the paucity of good walling of
any sort; in the same wall can be seen dark chocolate-brown
Greensand (known as Carstone), white, pink and bright-red
chalkstone or clunch, red bricks and grey and white flint cobbles.
The effect is rather messy but not altogether unpleasing,
particularly where the different coloured materials are arranged
in diaper or chequerboard patterns, as they sometimes are in the
larger buildings [37].

Carstone is also used in another way, with yellow or red brick
dressings, to form the main wall surface of the buildings. Minute
stones like bars of chocolate are used, the mortar being set well
back from the surface of the wall so that they look as though they
are laid dry. It is a sophisticated Victorian design technique,
light-hearted and attractive and using local materials, but hardly

qualifying as vernacular. Downham Market and Sandringham have excellent examples and interestingly enough there is at least one in Ely, which stands on its small outcrop of Greensand in the middle of the fen. Whether the carstone was brought from near Downham Market or was locally quarried we do not know. Victorian cottages of this sort, like so many Victorian cottages elsewhere, are roofed in Welsh slate.

Buildings in the north-east of the region are of brick, again with pantiled roofs and sloping dormers. Here the brick is reddy-brown, and it is here too that the crow-stepped and Dutch gables are most noticeable. Villages such as Worstead and Cawston show Continental influences in the rich brickwork of their weavers' cottages, recognisable by their comparative grandeur of scale. In the Broadlands the buildings are similar but generally roofed in reed thatch.

Dutch gables (Norfolk)

Pantiles do not often occur inland south of the Suffolk border, but along the coasts over much of Essex and Suffolk and in all of north Norfolk the pantile is universal, varying in colour from red in the north to brown in the south [38]. In Cambridgeshire, Norfolk and Suffolk, pantiles are mostly S-shaped, whereas in Essex the tile is traditionally of the flat-and-roll profile.

Pantiles were an innovation imported originally in the seventeenth century. They became popular not only because they were quicker to lay but because they made a lighter roof than plain tiles, which have to overlap three-deep to be watertight. Manufacture started in England towards the end of the eighteenth century. Their distribution is universal along the East Coast north of the Thames, all the way to Scotland. Pantiles were also imported into the South-west and many can be seen around the Bristol Channel. The standard pantile is laid at any pitch down to 30°, but most usually at 35° to 40° and at much steeper pitches when replacing thatch. Shiny, black-glazed pantiles were sometimes used and look extremely well on flint buildings; in fenland Cambridgeshire, pantiles are of a pale buff colour matching the pale buff bricks.

The brick buildings of the fenland islands and borders have a different appearance from those of the chalklands. Around Huntingdon the typical cottage is long and low, like its Lincolnshire neighbours, roofed in pale buff pantiles or in brindled plain tiles [46]. The brindled effect of the roofs is occasioned by the generally pale brown tiles being liberally mixed with buff tiles. The resulting pale 'heather-mixture' is surprisingly attractive and accords well with the pale brickwork, which is also rather speckly due to the variation in colour between the usually darker ends (headers) and paler sides (stretchers) of the bricks. Pale headers and dark stretchers can occasionally be seen, more particularly towards the Bedfordshire border; the effect is unusual and rather striking. The variation in colour between one side of the brick and another is due to the way the bricks are stacked in the kiln, usually so that the headers get burnt more thoroughly than the stretchers. Nearly all the fenland houses are pale, and generally buff in colour, an effect heightened by the local use of cream, buff or pale-brown paintwork.

The buildings of the valley lands of the south-east present an entirely different picture again. Here is a land originally covered in dense oak woods; all the older buildings are of timber with colour-washed plaster walls and plain-tiled roofs [48]. The typical Suffolk type of plastered and colour-washed house is often rather long, with complex roof-gable shapes over project-

Essex plaster and colour wash

ing first floors, known as jetties [43]. These jetties, or jutting out buildings, which are described more fully in Chapter 7, are made all of timber in the form of a box frame and are entirely plastered over with lime plaster, originally made with straw and dung to bind it, applied to the timber frame for insulation as well as for weatherproofing. The timbers were not intended to show (as they were all over the West of England and the Midlands) except in houses built before the sixteenth century, where the spaces between the timbers were filled with wattle-and-daub and the frame members were decoratively arranged. There is a tendency

Jettied timber cottage (Suffolk)

today to remove the plaster and expose the timbers, intended by their builders to be concealed, and this is a pity, not only because the building is made less waterproof but because the timbers were not tidily arranged and look ill-proportioned and irregular.

The plaster itself is very often decorated with raised patterns, a technique known as pargetting. Earlier examples, in comparatively high relief, are usually of conventional flowers or foliage, sometimes with figures, dates or initials [43]. By the eighteenth century, when taste was less flamboyant, the technique had retreated into a more polite low relief and patterns had become formalised and stereotyped, arranged in bands and frames to emphasise the building shape, the panels being sometimes left plain and sometimes filled with conventional combed patterns [44]. Pargetting is a famous feature of Suffolk, Cambridgeshire and parts of Essex and Hertfordshire and contributes notably to the plastered buildings of East Anglia.

Colour-wash in Suffolk is nearly all in the buff, yellow and apricot range of earth colours, and the village streets glow with their warm and sunny hues [44]. Pink too is a Suffolk speciality, but further west, in Hertfordshire and Cambridgeshire, white is more usual.

As in the Weald of Kent, there are many hall houses of early date in this region, but, unlike the Kentish examples, the East-Anglian hall house is roofed as three separate elements, the two end features having their roofs running at right angles to that of the main hall, giving the houses their many-gabled look. Sometimes the hall roof is at its original low level, but more often the roof has been raised to incorporate an upper floor, made possible by the introduction of a central chimney to carry away from the hearth the smoke which previously drifted up through the rafters and escaped via a vent in the roof [41].

Roofs in the valley country are nearly always made of plain tiles or thatch [42] and are almost invariably of gabled form, hardly ever with hips or half-hips.

Clay lump was used as an alternative walling material to timber all over the central part of the region, south-east of the brick and flint area. Clay lump is made of clay mixed with straw and formed into large building blocks jointed with clay mud and thickly plastered over to keep the clay dry. It is the English adobe. The walls are always built on a brick plinth as a protection against the damp, the plinth usually being tarred or painted black. Houses built of clay lump are subtly different in appearance from timber-framed houses, although like them they are covered with plaster. Houses in this region are nearly all whitewashed or colour-washed. The walls of clay need special protection from the damp, so roofs overhang at the eaves and verges have deep barge-boards, even in thatched houses. Most roofs in this style of house were originally thatched, so roof pitches are generally steep. Tall gable walls are in addition sometimes protected by sloping horizontal wooden ledges or shelves called 'pentice boards' [47]. These can be seen on timber buildings, as well as on those made of clay lump, all over the central southern part of the region. It is not easy to distinguish a

Peaked thatch and pentice boards (Cambridgeshire)

clay lump building from a timber one when both are plastered, wall thicknesses in the two materials being very similar, and, as the only sure way of telling is to drill a hole through the wall to see, it may be imagined that in most cases we have to be content with a guess, supported only by such features as the deep eaves and the overhanging barge-boards.

In Essex and Cambridgeshire the timber and white-plastered houses are similar to their Suffolk counterparts, but are generally simpler and often long and low with a single thatched gabled roof, peaked at the ends of the ridge like a Viking ship. These peaked ends to the thatch are a highly characteristic feature of Cambridge and Essex [45].

In south-east Essex weatherboarding is a common alternative to plaster. Weatherboarding became popular in the eighteenth and nineteenth centuries in eastern districts, as it did in Kent, and this may have been because of the brick tax or because it was cheaper than plastering and needed no great skill to fix on to the buildings. Weatherboarding in Essex is traditionally painted black or tarred, although the more conventional white-painted boards are often seen to-day. The material is not a good insulator and requires a lot of maintenance, but there is a strong tradition of building in weatherboarding, particularly towards the Essex and Hertfordshire border, the homeland of many of the New England settlers who carried the technique to more advanced lengths in the Colonial style of America [40].

The black and white painted weatherboards contrast well with the brownish-red plain-tiled roofs which, in the south-east of the region, are very often of Mansard form: a device for gaining more space in the roof storey. Pantiled roofs are seldom of this shape but, as suits their inflexible nature, are more often built with simple gables.

There is a type of small cottage which occurs in all the eastern counties. This is the modest one-and-a-half storey cottage with dormer windows to small bedrooms in the roof space, the roof covered with pantiles or plain tiles according to location [46]. In every case the proportions of the cottages are similar and they seem to suit the landscape wherever they occur. Their walling

Mansard roof (Essex)

material varies with their site: of brick in the fenlands, of limestone in the Lincolnshire hills, of flint in Norfolk, and of timber (plastered or weatherboarded) in Suffolk or Essex. Perhaps these cottages look their best in brick with pantiled roofs, set in the low, sweeping landscape of the fens.

East Anglia provides more variety in its building types than the map might lead one to expect. The lasting impressions of the region must be of the two dominant types of house: the glowing, many-gabled plastered and colour-washed houses of Suffolk, and the austere grey-and-yellow flint houses of Norfolk.

Norfolk cottages

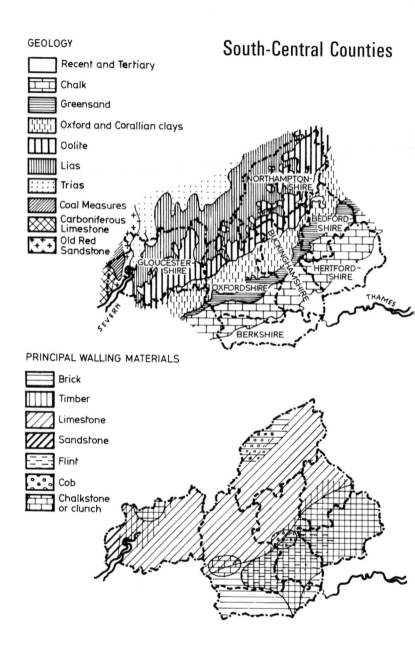

GEOLOGY

South-Central Counties

- Recent and Tertiary
- Chalk
- Greensand
- Oxford and Corallian clays
- Oolite
- Lias
- Trias
- Coal Measures
- Carboniferous Limestone
- Old Red Sandstone

NORTHAMPTON-SHIRE

BEDFORD-SHIRE

BUCKINGHAMSHIRE

GLOUCESTER-SHIRE

HERTFORD-SHIRE

OXFORDSHIRE

THAMES

SEVERN

BERKSHIRE

PRINCIPAL WALLING MATERIALS

- Brick
- Timber
- Limestone
- Sandstone
- Flint
- Cob
- Chalkstone or clunch

49

50

51

52

SOUTH-CENTRAL COUNTIES

49 Farnborough, BERKSHIRE. Red-brick cottages on the Berkshire Downs (*page 92*)
50 Cottered, HERTFORDSHIRE. White plastered row with a weatherboarded base (*page 94*)
51 Woolstone, near Wantage, OXFORDSHIRE. Fine clunch walling; brick arches replacing original timber lintels (*page 91*)
52 Amersham, BUCKINGHAMSHIRE. Eighteenth-century brick cottage row with segmental arches (*page 92*)

53

54

55

56

SOUTH-CENTRAL COUNTIES

53 Sapperton, GLOUCESTERSHIRE. A fine Cotswold house built in limestone rubble (*page 86*)

54 Stanton, GLOUCESTERSHIRE. A gabled Cotswold street (*page 84*)

55 Saintbury, GLOUCESTERSHIRE. A plain farmhouse built in ashlared stone and graded Cotswold slates (*page 87*)

56 Stanton, GLOUCESTERSHIRE. A classic Cotswold house type, with mullioned dormer windows in subsidiary gables (*page 84*)

57

58

59

60

SOUTH-CENTRAL COUNTIES

57 Apperley, GLOUCESTERSHIRE. A timber-framed house in the Severn Valley (*page 89*)

58 Swinbrook, OXFORDSHIRE. Simple limestone vernacular of the Cotswold borders (*page 86*)

59 Sibford Gower, OXFORDSHIRE. Steeply pitched thatch and rubble stone in the Redlands (*page 88*)

60 Eastleigh Turville, OXFORDSHIRE. A seventeenth-century house in the Cotswold tradition (*pages 82 & 88*)

61

62

63

64

SOUTH-CENTRAL COUNTIES

61 Collyweston, NORTHAMPTONSHIRE. A fine house with local stone roof and a two-storeyed bay window (*page 88*)

62 Badby, NORTHAMPTONSHIRE. The steep roofed Northamptonshire type (*page 88*)

63 Gretton, NORTHAMPTONSHIRE. A house in pale limestone with emphasis on the end gable (*page 84*)

64 East Haddon, NORTHAMPTONSHIRE. Banded stone and tall thatched roof (*page 88*)

6. South-Central Counties
Gloucestershire, Oxfordshire,
Northamptonshire, Berkshire,
Buckinghamshire, Bedfordshire and
Hertfordshire

Grey Stone and Red Brick

The region divides conveniently into three parts: the dominant area of limestone uplands in the centre, where the buildings are of stone; the small area west of the Cotswold escarpment, comprising the Vale country and the Forest of Dean, where building materials are mixed and the style of building is more like that of adjoining regions; and the large south-eastern part of the region, where the principal building material is brick.

First, the limestone country.

The valley of the upper Thames, together with its romantically named tributaries, Cherwell, Evenlode, Windrush and Colne, controls the drainage of the greater part of the region. Along the main river and for many miles on either hand is an open upland country of brimming streams meandering through flat windy meadows, bordered by poplars and willows; an unemphatic land of cool grey buildings and ancient grey bridges that westwards merges imperceptibly into the sterner, less smiling area of the southern Cotswolds, culminating in the level-topped hills and deep wooded valleys of the limestone scarplands overlooking the Severn.

Northwards, there is no such gradual change in character, for the grey oolite of the Cotswolds gives place quite suddenly to the brown and orange marlstone of north Oxfordshire and the Northamptonshire hills. This, the Liassic limestone, gives the countryside quite a different look. No longer the cool greys of the open valleys and bare hills: here the country, known as the Redlands, is more hilly and tumbled and the fields are red and brown; the land is rich mixed farming; fields are hedged (not walled, as in the Cotswolds), and the buildings are yellow, brown and thatched.

Beyond the Redlands to the north, the Northamptonshire limestones continue, brown and rusty-coloured, sometimes tinged with green. This is the great iron-producing area around Corby. Here we are over the watershed and the land drains towards the Wash by the three rivers Welland, Nene and Ouse.

The Cotswold hills form architecturally the most interesting part of the region, for the Cotswold style of building is the archetype for the whole of the limestone belt. The best building stones come from the triangular area between Stroud, Burford and Chipping Campden. Here the oolite is easily cut and dressed and has given rise to a fine traditional craftsmanship. The region remained rich for a long time, so that the splendid techniques of building in limestone could be fully developed and even quite humble cottages were normally built of this beautiful material from the seventeenth century onwards.

The wealth of the Cotswolds came from sheep, as it did in so many rural areas of England. The fourteenth and fifteenth centuries saw the peak of the wool trade's prosperity in the area and many fine houses in such towns as Chipping Campden and Northleach were built at that time. The bulk of the smaller houses and cottages are however of the seventeenth and eighteenth centuries, by which time the wool-weaving industry had been firmly established along the small streams in the steep wooded valleys of the escarpment.

Buildings must be regarded in relation not only to their location but their date. Generally in the Cotswolds, the earlier the date the steeper the pitch of the roof [60]. Also, since in earlier centuries the humbler cottages were not yet built in stone, the earlier buildings that have survived are inevitably the grander. So it is that in the larger farms and manors, and particularly in merchants' town houses, we see all the trappings of late medieval prosperity: the parapetted gable, the finial on top, the elaborate mullioned window, and the four-centred arches over the doorways, with their rectangular drip-stones or labels forming decorative triangular spaces in the corners. Later examples are simpler or, conversely, cottages are generally later. (It must be remembered that sophisticated Georgian and Palladian town houses in such wealthy communities as Painswick are not included in our survey of the vernacular.)

Cotswold town house

These simpler and later houses however have many universal characteristics. Primarily they have gabled and stone-slated roofs, pitched from 45° to 50°, with small eaves and plain verges. Their upper-floor rooms are in the roof space, having partially sloping ceilings, and are lit by windows in minor subsidiary gables, which are taken up in stonework in the same face as the main wall. Windows often have stone mullions supporting stone lintels with drip-stones over [56]. In the classical Cotswold area wooden lintels are seen only in the humbler cottages, and throughout the area chimneys are located at the ends of the buildings.

Cotswold dormer windows

Frames in stone-mullioned windows are almost invariably made of wrought iron. This is particularly so in the Cotswolds, where late medieval traditional craft techniques became so deeply rooted. Frames are narrow and fixed lights are frequently glazed straight into grooves in the stone without a frame at all, so that mullioned windows seem all stone and glass. Further north in the Redlands of Oxfordshire and Northamptonshire timber frames, usually painted white, are more often seen.

Particularly in the north Cotswolds, gable walls are often treated as a decorative feature, with windows arranged in an ascending sequence of diminishing lights, as four lights on the ground floor, three on the first and two in the roof space, which makes a satisfying if rather contrived pattern [63]. Ashlar, or sawn and finely jointed rectangular stonework, is common and ashlared corner stones, chimneys and window dressings are universal even where walling is in rubble. The secondary gables with their dormer windows are a more important feature of the Cotswold scene than any other. They provide a varied skyline to the terraces and rows of cottages that give the village streets their distinctive character [54].

The whole technique of building mullioned and drip-stoned

A Cotswold village

windows is medieval in concept but, due to the powerful influence of traditional craft practice, remained in force until well into the eighteenth century. As it was dying out, the nineteenth-century revivalist movement reactivated the style. Thus, in the Cotswolds, building techniques remained in force from the Middle Ages until well into modern times.

One particular feature of the Cotswold scene which above all else affects its character is the virtual invisibility of the buildings. This is due to the universal use of the same material, which itself assumes the same tone as its background. Entire villages and whole small towns are constructed wholly of oolitic limestone, without a brick, a slate or any other foreign intruder being present. Of few other localities can it be said that the buildings, their walls, windows, roofs and chimneys (and, until comparatively recently, their footways and road surfaces), are all of the same material. The field walls, at least in the high Cotswolds, are also of the oolite. The roofs, being exposed to the rain, gather moss and lichen and thus are rather darker in tone than the walls; but the walls, being vertical, receive less light and thus appear to be of much the same tone as the roofs. On a dull day, when there are no shadows, whole villages seem to melt into the landscape. This is what makes painting and photographing the Cotswold scene so difficult. Almost everybody likes and admires the Cotswolds; few have successfully recorded them.

For the most part the houses of the Cotswolds are in the villages and the villages are in the many sudden little valleys that intersect their bleaker upland fields. Towards the scarplands above Stroud however the valleys are chasms hundreds of feet deep, filled with dense woods, wild and waterlogged. Here the villages have to occupy the hilltops, as at Sapperton, Oakridge and Minchinhampton [53]. Lower down the valleys, mills occupy the restricted valley floors, and the unpretentious houses, mostly eighteenth- and nineteenth-century, climb up the precipitous hillsides in terraces of stone, colour-wash or render, the terraces connected by steep little stepped alleyways negotiated, almost until the Second World War, by donkeys which carried panniers for delivering the bread.

Stroud Valley mills (Gloucestershire)

The buildings of the Oxford plain are simpler and more straightforward than those of the Cotswolds. These buildings have fewer secondary gables than in the Cotswolds proper but many more small gabled dormers in the roof. Mullioned windows are comparatively rare and doors and windows generally have long oak lintels [58]. The stonework of the Oxford plain is small in scale and rubbly, derived for the most part from the Cornbrash or the Corallian. Only west of Oxford are roofs generally of stone slates; east of Oxford most buildings, although of stone, are roofed in plain tiles.

The almost universal use since the fourteenth and fifteenth centuries of stone slates throughout the western oolite areas in this region calls for comment. (The roofer is called a 'slater' or 'slatter', so 'tile' would be an inappropriate name, although it is sometimes used in this connection.) The slates are got locally in very many cases, but the most famous centres for production were Stonesfield near Woodstock and Collyweston in the extreme north of Northamptonshire. Slates from each source look much the same and are got from the sandy strata of the oolite which the quarrymen call 'the pendle'. If anything, the Northamptonshire slates are somewhat larger, thinner and more regular in colour and texture, whereas the Cotswold slates provide a more interesting and grainy roof [55]. All slates are graded from large slabs at the eaves to tiny pieces at the ridge, but, generally speaking, the stone slate is a small roofing unit and so is capable of being manipulated in a more plastic manner than, say, the Welsh slates or pantiles. This makes it possible to use secondary gables and dormers and to sweep the slates round the internal angle, which is not only pleasing to the eye but avoids the use of clumsy valley gutters.

Towards the north of Oxfordshire in the Redlands, and into Northamptonshire, the architecture changes. Here on the Lias the stone is yellow, brown and orange and is quarried in squarer, lumpier pieces which contrast with the paler colour of the mortar

A high pitched Northamptonshire roof

so that individual stones are much more apparent than on the oolite, where the stones merge together in a way that heightens the homogeneous appearance of the Cotswold houses [60]. In the Redlands thatch is an almost universal roofing material [59], but, unlike the thatched cottages of Hampshire, these are tall, two-storeyed buildings, their roofs pitched up higher and higher as we go further into Northamptonshire [62]. Parapetted gables are common; these are usually corbelled out at the eaves to protect the end of the roof overhang. The gabled ends of the houses often face the street to save space in crowded villages.

Further north, near Collyweston, roofs are again of stone slates. Other features of the district are the gabled bay windows and double stone chimney-stacks, seen in the earlier and wealthier houses [61].

Gabled bay window at Collyweston

Paler grey oolite is quarried in the eastern and northern parts of Northamptonshire, and many houses of the borderlands between grey and brown limestone have decorative walling in alternate bands of dark and light [64]. These can be seen, for instance, at Culworth and Gretton. Up the waterways of the Welland, Nene and Ouse, from the eastern ports, came the pantiles. Along these rivers, where the grey limestone predominates, a marked similarity with the houses of Yorkshire and Lincolnshire is apparent: simple, gabled, grey stone buildings with warm brown and red pantiled roofs.

The second part of the region lies beyond the Cotswold escarpment in the west, where the land plunges down six hundred feet and more to the Severn Valley. The ancient and varied geology of the valley floor gives rise to a rich agricultural landscape in which brick, timber and stone buildings are common. North of Gloucester, on both sides of the Severn, orchards and market gardens are reminiscent of the Vale of Evesham, which the area adjoins, and the buildings are of brick and timber, following the black-and-white tradition of the western Midlands [57].

The broad Severn winds through this vale country, its tidal waters revealing huge stretches of gleaming sand and mud. Along the banks built high against the treacherous floods, and beside the two canals which intersect at Saul (the ship canal and the earlier Thames and Severn Junction), houses have the flavour of canal cottages everywhere: eighteenth- and early nineteenth-century brick houses with segmental brick arches to doors and windows, built in rows with low-pitched roofs, here covered with pantiles brought up the Severn from Bridgwater to Framilode, Sharpness and Gloucester.

Across the water in Newnham, a curiosity of a few of the riverside houses is the material of their lower storeys. Newnham was a great shipbuilding place in the days of wooden sailing ships and a minor port for the iron and coal industry of the Forest of Dean, so the riverside houses have an air of antique industry and some are converted warehouses, possibly rope-walks. Large blocks of furnace slag are used as walling material in these buildings. The blocks are dark chocolate-brown and have a deeply convoluted texture, but they are cast to a true face and are, into the bargain, distinctly iridescent—a truly vernacular curiosity and an excellent minor example of the use of whatever material is at hand.

In the Vale of Gloucester, the houses are built of all and every material, reflecting the mixed and varied geology. Timber and bricks are perhaps the most common, some with plain-tiled roofs and some with pantiles. A feature of the neighbourhood is the external chimney-stack which, built of brick or stone, is sometimes so large that it dwarfs the house it serves. These stacks are built outside the timber houses to guard against fire—a plan entirely different from that adopted in Suffolk, where the timber houses surround the large central stacks on which the house timbers rest. We are here on the boundary of the West-Central region described in Chapter 7, where the huge external chimney is an important feature of the vernacular style.

Large external chimney (Vale of Gloucester)

Further west again lies the Forest of Dean, that strange, isolated and individual area of steep oak woods, ancient bracken-covered workings, coal-tips and scattered active industry. Carboniferous rocks yield sandstones (like the soft Pennant stone, which is a pale, greenish-grey), and round the edges of the central dome there are brown and pink sandstones of which many old farmhouses are made. The generality of buildings in the Forest are of more recent date and their modest stone walls, nearly always whitewashed or colour-washed, are quite reminiscent of Wales.

Finally, the large south-eastern area of the region.

Whitewashed cottage (Forest of Dean)

Below Oxford, open flat valley country lies below the Chalk escarpment, and here beneath the Berkshire Downs and the Chilterns runs the inevitable narrow band of Greensand, although its use in this area as a building stone is comparatively rare. Beneath the scarp, in addition to the universal brick, it is the Chalk itself that makes the more conspicuous contribution. Along the foot of the Berkshire Downs, notably at Uffington, clunch blocks from the lower Chalk have been most successfully and delightfully used until quite recently [51]. There are also some famous clunch quarries at Tottenhoe near Dunstable. Around Aylesbury there is to be found a chalk and clay mixture suitable for making cob, which is here called 'wichert'; buildings of this material are plastered and colour-washed and have small windows. Nearly all the buildings of the Greensand belt are thatched or plain-tiled, the thatch in the area becoming rarer as the cost of replacement and upkeep continues to rise. Apart from occasional clunch, wichert or Greensand examples, red brick is paramount.

All over the chalk hills of Buckinghamshire and Berkshire, red bricks and red tiles predominate. It is a typical chalkland country of beech woods and yew trees, of dry valleys and smoothly contoured fields, through which the Thames cuts at Goring, bringing to the villages round Henley, Marlow and Maidenhead a riparian atmosphere that combines unexpectedly with that of the chalk hills behind.

The brickwork of this wealthy area is of a high quality. Red, grey and blue bricks are used with a consistency and elegance scarcely matched elsewhere in England [49]. South Buckinghamshire and Berkshire share this tradition of fine brickwork, which imparts a fresh, bright character to all the little country towns, sparkling in their fresh white paint, which sets off their warm-coloured bricks and tiles [52]. There is a type of vitrified

Georgian brick houses at Amersham (Buckinghamshire)

silver-grey brick, much used in the eighteenth century, which was made at Nettlebed and other places near Henley and Reading, and browny-red bricks are used all over the Chilterns around Amersham. Most of the houses in the wealthy areas of the Chilterns and Thames-side are of eighteenth-century date and display many attractive eighteenth-century features in their brickwork, such as diaper patterns made by the careful arrangement of the shiny, blueish overburnt ends of the bonding bricks (headers), or nicely laid segmental brick arches (one, two or three bricks deep) over doors and windows, or, again, quoins executed in bricks selected for their slightly darker or lighter shade.

Flint walling occurs sporadically over all the downlands, but to nothing like the extent that it does in Norfolk and the South Downs. Chalkland houses are typically of warm red brick with red and brown plain-tiled roofs—comfortable, snug and small. Many older houses in the little towns in and near the chalklands have timber frames infilled with brick. Houses are usually arranged with their eaves parallel to the street, without subsidiary gables, so a village street in this part of the region presents an entirely different picture to the many-gabled serration of a similar street in a Cotswold village. Windows and door frames are painted white or green; doorways have little porches in wood or metal trellis. The accent is on simple domesticity, not aggressively rural in character, with few frills and of good quality.

East of the Chilterns, the chalklands become more and more obscured by overlying layers of clays and gravels, and the dimpled countryside of east Hertfordshire, with its wooded valleys and rounded hills (a countryside of mists, foregrounds and close-ups, like a Chinese scroll painting), becomes more East Anglian in the character of its buildings as the borders of Essex and south Cambridgeshire are approached. Here, bricks give way to timber, plaster, whitewash and weatherboarding.

The East Anglian style of building has been described in Chapter 5. Hertfordshire is a transitional county, lying midway between the brick traditions of the Thames Valley and the Chilterns and the timber traditions of East Anglia, and shows clearly in its buildings the influences of both regions. A curious feature of some Hertfordshire plastered buildings is the weatherboarded plinth—a long strip of weatherboarding, often painted black, along the base of the whitewashed plastered houses

Black weatherboarded plinth (Hertfordshire)

[50]. The wholly weatherboarded buildings, most of them to be seen in the south-east of the county, are similar to those of Essex, and reference has been made to the affinities with the North American Colonial style in the preceding chapter. Further into Bedfordshire and north Buckinghamshire the brick traditions of the region persist, but here, in addition to reds, the clays provide paler bricks. This gives a distinct flavour of Cambridgeshire to the countryside, especially to the north-east, where the flat lands begin. Pale yellow, buff and browny-grey bricks predominate and roofs are plain-tiled or occasionally thatched.

In nineteenth-century cottages, bricklayers sometimes laid their bricks on edge. This method uses fewer bricks and makes a lighter wall with cavities between the bricks. The appearance of the brickwork, sometimes called Chinese or 'rat-trap' bond, is rather disconcerting, as the larger brick face reduces the scale of the buildings, so that they look like dolls' houses. The pale bricks of the north-eastern part of the region are the product of the limey Jurassic clays which blanket the valleys adjoining the Chalk and the Oolite, and of the Gault clays that occur in the Greensand.

The immense deposits of brick clay in Bedfordshire and Buckinghamshire have given rise to some of the largest modern brickworks in England, mostly producing 'common' bricks for interior use. Before these great brickworks were established however the area produced a brindled brick, not unlike that of Huntingdon, and this can be seen in some of the older cottages of the area.

Among all this wide variety of colours and types of brickwork it is nevertheless the red bricks which have pride of place. Red bricks and warm-tiled roofs in their green and comfortable setting make a lasting picture of a very English part of England.

This wide and varied region of the South-Central counties occupies a central position and links the country from the Bristol Channel to the London Basin and from the Berkshire Downs to the rivers of the Wash; it embraces the principal area of the limestone belt and relates to the true Midlands of England.

7. West-Central Counties

Herefordshire and Worcestershire, Warwickshire, Salop, Staffordshire and Cheshire

The Home of Black and White Buildings

The region has a highly individual character and much of it is due to the geological consistency of its low-lying areas, nearly all sandstones and clays which gave rise in the past to dense oak woods. This character is made more interesting by the unexpectedness of the many abrupt, isolated hill masses that are scattered seemingly at random throughout the western half of the region.

By contrast, the character of the highland areas, which occupy the region's boundaries, is more akin to that of its neighbours.

The West-central region is like a long dish with raised edges represented by the Pennines, the Cotswolds and the mountains of Wales, but open to the north, where the Cheshire Plain rolls on clear across the Ship Canal into Lancashire, and to the south, where the wide valley of the Severn cuts between Gloucester and Wales. In the south-east the Stratford Avon, which has its head-waters in Northamptonshire, forms the broad Vale of Evesham.

The floor of the dish is a rolling, rural countryside of rich farms, traversed by a truly impressive number of rivers—Severn, Avon and Teme; Wye, Arrow and Frome, and, in the north, Dee and Weaver. Even the young Trent makes a brief appearance in Staffordshire in the north-east. In the middle of the dish is the huge conurbation of the West Midlands.

The region can be divided into three main parts: the south-west area, embraced by the loop of the Severn, which travels

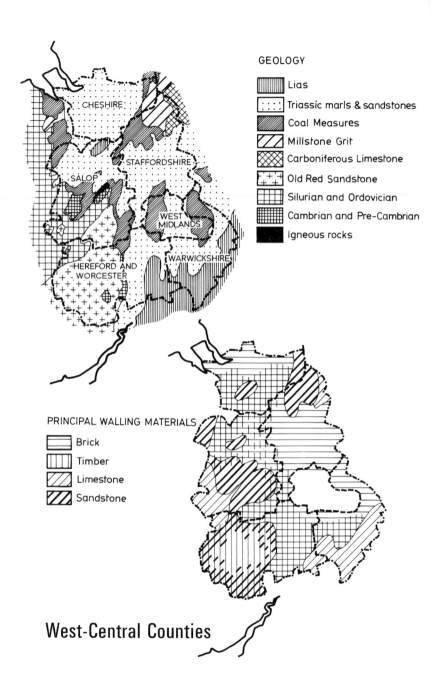

GEOLOGY

- ▨ Lias
- ⣿ Triassic marls & sandstones
- ▨ Coal Measures
- ▨ Millstone Grit
- ▨ Carboniferous Limestone
- ⊞ Old Red Sandstone
- ⊞ Silurian and Ordovician
- ⊞ Cambrian and Pre-Cambrian
- ■ Igneous rocks

CHESHIRE

STAFFORDSHIRE

SALOP

WEST MIDLANDS

WARWICKSHIRE

HEREFORD AND WORCESTER

PRINCIPAL WALLING MATERIALS

- ▭ Brick
- ▥ Timber
- ▨ Limestone
- ▨ Sandstone

West-Central Counties

65

66

67

68

WEST-CENTRAL COUNTIES

65 Old Marton Hall, near Ellesmere, SALOP. A magnificent stone-roofed farmhouse with a two-storeyed porch (*page 104*)

66 Hughley, SALOP. A large timber-framed farmhouse (*page 99*)

67 Weobley, HEREFORDSHIRE. Jettied post-and-truss buildings (*pages 98 & 102*)

68 Hordley, SALOP. A farmhouse with huge timbers and square panels (*page 98*)

69

70

71

WEST-CENTRAL COUNTIES

69 Near Diddlebury, SALOP. A beautifully sited farm on Wenlock Edge, built of yellow limestone (*page 105*)

70 Worfield, SALOP. A modest timber-framed cottage (*page 98*)

71 Jackfields, SALOP. The large dark bricks and massive chimneys of the industrial area round Coalbrookdale (*page 105*)

72

73

74

75

WEST-CENTRAL COUNTIES

72 Near Marton, CHESHIRE. Brindled brickwork of the north Cheshire plain (*page 104*)
73 Fullers Moor, CHESHIRE. Cottages of large New Red Sandstone blocks (*page 105*)
74 Langley, Macclesfield, CHESHIRE. Pale-buff local sandstone and large stone slates from the Coal Measures (*page 106*)
75 Alstonfield, STAFFORDSHIRE. A Pennine farmhouse with dark-purple plain tiles from the Potteries (*pages 106 & 129*)

76

77

78

79

WEST-CENTRAL COUNTIES

76 Pebworth, WORCESTERSHIRE. The more intimate scale of thatched black-and-white cottages in the Vale of Evesham (*page 107*)

77 Kineton, WARWICKSHIRE. The severe style of a Lias stone farmhouse (*page 108*)

78 Ombersley, WORCESTERSHIRE. An elegant example of cruck construction (*pages 101 & 107*)

79 Exhall, WARWICKSHIRE. Unpainted timber buildings also occur in the region (*page 107*)

eastwards across the middle before turning south between Ironbridge and Bridgnorth (where timber is the main building material); the eastern area of Warwickshire, Worcestershire and south Staffordshire, dominated inevitably by the Black Country and the influence of the West Midlands (where building materials are mixed—brick, timber and stone); and the northern area of north Salop and the Cheshire Plain (where the predominating building material is brick). Each area has its own isolated, quirky hills, where the buildings are of stone.

Geologically, the region is almost all Red Sandstone: hard, dark Old Red Sandstone in the south-west; soft, paler New Red Sandstone in the north and east. The sandstones are for the most part heavily overlain with marls, clays and recent glacial deposits which give rise to rich dairy-farming country.

Out of the lowland sandstones protrude the abrupt hills of ancient rock: the Malverns, which divide the Old and New Sandstones like a wall; The Wrekin, which stands like a sentinel in the plain between the Pennines and the Welsh mountains; the Clee Hills and Wenlock Edge.

In the north, no less abrupt but smaller hills of the Red Sandstone itself occur, such as Nescliffe, Helsby and Beeston, with its fabulous grey fairy-tale medieval castle.

The Welsh Marches are a transitional area of steep, tumbled foothills and broad valleys, a land of crags and castles where the gentle countryside of England merges with the scenery of Wales. Here, among the brackeny hills, buildings are of stone. The character of the buildings is as transitional as the landscape, and a marked Welsh flavour is noticeable.

In the south-west area the relatively few arable fields are red, purple-brown or pink, the sandstone churches are red or dark grey with lichen, the pastures are deep green, the commonest trees are oak and holly. This is a well watered, well wooded, deep green landscape of fields and hedges, woods and coppices, ponds and streams; a dark toned, quiet and peaceful landscape of small-scale hills and vales. In contrast, the brilliant magpie of the black-and-white buildings set against such a background, whether seen at a distance sparkling over the trees and hedges or

seen nearby at the roadside, gives just the necessary astringency
to a scene otherwise almost oppressively verdant.

Large black and white farmhouse (Worcestershire)

Black-and-white architecture, the hall-mark of the west
Midlands, occurs all over the region, but nowhere more
consistently or universally than in Herefordshire and the south-
west. Here a truly remarkable scene meets the eye, where village
after village is entirely built of black-and-white houses [67],
primitive and antique in appearance and massively out of plumb,
their huge timbers widely spaced, raised on heavy stone bases,
their roofs low-pitched and overhanging. Eighteenth- and
nineteenth-century houses too are built of timber, or, so strong is
the black-and-white tradition, have been painted to simulate
timber structures with black-painted bands on white painted
brickwork.

The forests in this part of England were cleared later than in
other districts and consequently the tradition of building in
timber persisted until a comparatively recent date. The timber
buildings of the West are of quite a different character to those of
the East of England. Here the structures are more massive-
looking, more robust in appearance, certainly more exhuberant
and showy. Unlike the wooden houses of East Anglia that are
covered all over with plaster, or the houses of Kent and Sussex
which are clad in weatherboarding or hung tiles, these buildings
were designed for their timbers to be seen, the spaces between
being filled with heavily plastered wattle-and-daub or brick, the
infill in either case being whitewashed.

The fashion for painting the infill white appears to be of a fairly respectable age, but that for blackening the timbers seems more open to question in this respect. Some authorities hold that blackening the timbers was only practised from the nineteenth century and others would put the date much earlier. However that may be, we enjoy the result.

In the south of the region the patterns made by the black timbers on their white background are simple squares [66]. Further north, the timbering becomes more elaborate and closely spaced, until the black woodwork is used not only as a structure but as a decoration, the natural squares and triangles of the structure being filled with quatrefoils and zig-zags, curves and criss-crosses—a somewhat tasteless exuberance consistent with the flamboyance of the late Tudor, Elizabethan and early Stuart ages in which so many of the larger houses were built.

Ornate patterns in timber (near Shrewsbury)

The form of these houses is totally unlike that of the timber houses of Kent and Sussex of similar date, which have central chimneys and overall hipped roofs, but there is some similarity with the houses of East Anglia, in so far as the earlier houses have their two end wings at right angles to the line of the main part of the building, forming gables on the street side. The similarity however ends there.

The most noticeable feature of the West Country houses is the external chimney stack. This is virtually universal and is enormous. It is built in stone or brick, or often in a combination of the two, the upper flue being constructed of brick (the more manageable material for making the thin part of the chimney). At the base, the chimney widens out to form the hearth, the chimney corner and the oven. The chimneys are built outside and independent of the timber structure for two main reasons. One is to minimise the fire risk. But perhaps the more fundamental reason (since many chimneys elsewhere are successfully built inside timber buildings) is that the timber structure was framed together by the house wrights in houses like these in such a way that its timbers could not be interrupted by the introduction of a hole in floor or roof large enough to receive a chimney.

Huge outside chimney stack (Herefordshire)

There are two basic sorts of timber structure (and it must be emphasised that timber buildings are *structures*, like Meccano; the walls are added or infilled later; quite a different concept to a building of masonry or brick). Firstly there is the structure where the roof is carried on a series of two or more frames which rest upon the ground, and secondly there is the structure where the roof rests continuously upon walls made of a pallisade of uprights.

The simplest form of the first sort is the cruck building [78]. Here two or more crucks are assembled flat on the ground (each pair comprising two huge bent timbers, matched by using the two split or sawn halves of the same log) and then 'reared', pairs of crucks being about sixteen feet (4.8 m) apart. The distance between pairs of crucks is called the 'bay' and is supposed to be governed by the space required for four oxen. Small cottages might be one bay only in length; larger buildings of two, three or four bays. The width or span of the crucks, and hence the width of the buildings, was usually about eighteen feet (5.5 m). Each pair of crucks is joined and stiffened with a cross-piece or tie and is joined to the next pair with longitudinal timbers called plates and purlins, the plates resting on the ties. Diagonal bracing timbers are inserted to provide lengthwise stability. The roof and walls can be built after the structure is complete.

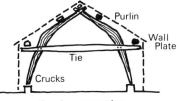

Cruck construction

It is interesting to see that this method of building, often held up to be the most primitive, enables the walls to be totally independent of the structure in precisely the same way that steel and concrete techniques do to-day. It would be quite feasible in a cruck building to provide a heavy roof and no walls at all. Many cruck buildings can be seen to-day all over the west Midland counties, the crucks nearly always showing on the end walls.

The other basic timber structure is the box frame. Here tie beams perform a different function, stabilising the walls and preventing the spread of the roof. They rest upon the wall plates rather than vice versa. In older houses the tie was often a true beam upon which supporting members of the roof could rest, while in later and less massively built houses the tie became much lighter.

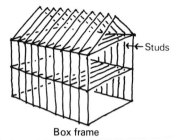

Box frame

Unlike the southern and eastern parts of England, in this part of the country the box frame principle is hardly used at all and a third system, which can be regarded as a development of the first, is almost universal for larger buildings. This structural system is called 'post and truss'. The truss is an A frame which rests on heavy posts, the frames and posts being spaced out ten to fifteen feet apart and joined together with a longitudinal floor beam and purlins. The heavy roof rests on the purlins in the same way as in a cruck building. The walls between the posts have no structural function other than as stiffeners and so can be treated decoratively. In this type of construction the ends of the purlins can always be seen on the gable ends of the houses unless covered by a barge-board. Post-and-truss building lends itself better than cruck building to jettying out the first floor, a technique which had its origins in towns where ground space was scarce and which was adopted all over England for timber buildings in the late Middle Ages—in country districts, presumably because of its attractive and fashionable appearance [67].

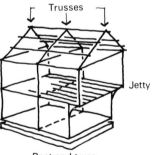

Post and truss

The West Country has many jettied buildings, some as late as the seventeenth century. It is the intricacy and complications of such timber buildings, in which their owners and builders so evidently revelled, that is their chief appeal to-day, perhaps even more so because of the huge timbers used.

A good deal of emphasis has been placed on the way the structural system transmits the roof load to the ground, and this is a very important consideration in view of the enormous weight of the stone slates in this part of the country. The roofs are of sandstone slabs derived from the Old Red Sandstone of Herefordshire, from the Ordovician and Silurian rocks of the Welsh borderlands and from the Coal Measures of the north-eastern part of the region.

Roofs are laid at a low pitch, sometimes down to 30°, the stones used being much larger and heavier and somewhat smoother than the limestone slates of the Cotswolds. Here the refinement of limestone roofs is missing. Low pitches combined with simple shapes, few dormers and a complete lack of hips: these are the chief characteristics of the West Country stone roof.

One of the features of the larger and earlier timber farmhouses is the two-storeyed porch, rather like a wooden version of the

Two-storeyed timber porch (Salop)

gabled bay window of the limestone area of north Northamptonshire [65].

Timber buildings with plastered infill panels require a lot of protection from the rain, so eaves and verges have a good overhang and barge-boards are common.

The northern area of the region, comprising all of Cheshire and part of north Salop and Staffordshire, is primarily a region of brick buildings, although plenty of larger and older houses are of timber in the full black-and-white tradition.

Bricks in Cheshire are a beautiful, dusky red-brown, sufficiently variable in colour to give the buildings a slightly brindled appearance that is most seductive [72]. Here on the Cheshire plain stand the large, prosperous dairy farms, their roofs of plain tiles or stone slates from Macclesfield (less often of Welsh slates), their walls of warm brick and with segmental brick arches to windows and doors. It is a scene of peace and rural prosperity which accords oddly with the stunning acres of modern technology writhing up into the sky at the refineries along the south bank of the Mersey, or with the delicate lacework of steel supporting the giant radio dish of Jodrell Bank.

Wherever the sandstone breaks through the overlying clays and sediments, it is used for building. Large blocks can be got from this easily cut material, which here, in the north part of the region, is a variable but strong orangey or brown-pink. Many

Pink sandstone cottages (Cheshire)

cottages can be seen built with carefully jointed blocks so big that they seem to dwarf these small buildings [73]. Farmyard and churchyard walls and farm out-buildings are more often built of sandstone than the houses; perhaps the stone is too porous for comfort.

In between the northern and south-western areas of the region lie the hills of the Coal Measures, the high ground of the Wyre Forest and the hills around Ironbridge, through which the Severn cuts its dramatic wooded gorge. Here, where the foundries of Coalbrookdale have blackened the buildings, roofs are of dark plain tiles, bricks are dark and the houses sombre as a consequence. Some recent cleaning reveals the bricks as a pleasant ruddy brown, but the local aesthetic, however transient, leans definitely towards the darker and richer colours. The bricks here are large, a full 3 inches (75 mm), compared with the southern English bricks of $2\frac{5}{8}$ inches (66 mm), and this slight difference does contribute towards the general air of sobriety and dignity by giving the buildings a subtly grander scale [71].

Over towards the west lies the double ridge of Wenlock Edge, where the buildings are of a pale grey, almost lemon-grey, limestone [69]. As in all limestone districts, Wenlock Edge produces pleasing buildings, but this is not the same limestone as the Oolite of the Cotswolds, nor even the same as the much earlier carboniferous limestone of the Pennines, but is a far older Silurian limestone which gives the buildings a simple character of their own, neither so grand as in the Cotswolds nor so classically serene as in the Pennines. Roofs in this district are of stone slates from the Hoar Edge area west of Much Wenlock.

Beyond Wenlock Edge, towards Wales, lie Caer Caradoc and the Long Mynd, and further south the large lump of Clun Forest. This is Marcher country, wild hills and pretty valleys with stone-built houses of every colour from purply brown to pale buff. Stone here is hard and most walling is of rubble; roofs are of slate, only occasionally of stone. Beyond the Long Mynd lie the lead hills called Stipperstones, with their curious shattered tors of dark green-grey rock and their weirdly deserted lead mines. From these heights, to descend to the valley bottom is to enter another world of cosy brick farms and deep meadows bordering the Severn.

It often comes as a surprise how much of the Pennines, and more particularly of the Peak District, lies in Cheshire and Staffordshire. In the north-east of the region, above Mac-clesfield, the steep hills are of Millstone Grit, and houses in cotton towns like Bollington are of the buff-grey sandstones of the Coal Measures, the older buildings roofed with dark grey sandstone slabs [74], the later ones in slate, for there was an excellent system of canals linking this area with North Wales. The gritstone houses of the moors above are reminiscent of those of Derbyshire and of the Yorkshire moors above Halifax and Huddersfield: large rectangular blocks of dark stone, stone mullions, low-pitched roofs and isolated farms.

Beyond the grit towards the east, the hills rise up to the Carboniferous Limestone and we can look down across the Derbyshire border into Dovedale. (The contrast between gritstone and limestone buildings is one of the chief delights of Derbyshire and the Yorkshire Dales, but to dwell upon this region here would be to anticipate Chapter 9.)

All around the Potteries and the upper waters of the Trent the tradition of brick- and tile-making from the abundant Trias clays is strong. In particular, the roofs of the buildings all the way up the Derbyshire border and down towards Stafford are of plain tiles, but plain tiles of a most unusual dark purply colour [75]. On the large brick farms, and particularly on the pale limestone buildings of the Derbyshire border, these shiny dark mauve roofs are a surprise and a delight.

Bricks in and around the Potteries are black from a century or more of soot; further south near Stafford the bricks are a remarkable dark purple; further east near Lichfield, of a no less striking pale, washed-out dusty red. But among all these colour variations it is the large size of the bricks, as around Ironbridge, that give these Midlands buildings their slightly ponderous character.

Worcestershire is essentially a brick county, the bricks being dark red for the most part. Here roofs are of plain tiles, red like

Staffordshire brick farmhouse

the bricks, or of thatch. Older cottages are of red brick and timber, the timber being sometimes blackened and sometimes left its natural browny colour [79]. Villages by the Teme and the Severn combine an antiquity of style with many Victorian buildings and are anything but sleepy.

There is little doubt that Warwickshire and Worcestershire look to Birmingham as their centre of gravity; nevertheless, there is a strong feeling of being pulled in two directions all over the northern parts of these counties, where the social, physical and economic influence of the West Midlands is keenly felt and where yet the Middle Ages never seem far away. Indeed, in spite of the area's all-pervading red-brick character, there are many small towns and villages, such as Ombersely, where the older western tradition of black-and-white buildings persists [78].

Further east and south, around Stratford, on the broad flood plain of the Avon, houses are again of red brick or black-and-white, thatched and cosy [76]. In this eastern area of the region houses are built of many materials, perhaps the most unexpected being stone from the Blue Lias. This outcrops in the south-west of Warwickshire. The stone here produces the same feeling in the buildings as it does in Somerset: the hard, even courses of horizontal stones, the mortar darker than the walls and the long stone lintels, all in cold greys or whites, as much of a contrast to the soft, thatched and half-timbered cottages of traditional

A homely Warwickshire cottage

Warwickshire as it would be possible to imagine [77]. The white stone is a rather pleasanter variant of the blue and can be seen with brown marlstone mullions, quoins and dressings, a more pleasing contrast than the equivalent brighter yellow Ham Hill stone of Somerset with the cold Blue Lias.

Nearer the edge of the limestone escarpment which forms the southern rim of our region, houses are built of the yellow-brown upland marlstone and look much like the houses over the border in Northamptonshire and in the Redlands of Oxfordshire.

We have journeyed clockwise round this varied region, starting in the south-west in the deeply rural countryside of Herefordshire, round the top of the region above Macclesfield and down the eastern side into Warwickshire. Although the hilly fringes and surroundings of the region produce many variations, the lowland centre has one consistent feature: its black-and-white timber buildings.

8. East-Central Counties
Leicestershire, Lincolnshire, Nottinghamshire and Humberside

Pantiles, Brick and Limestone

Although brick is the principal building material of the generally low-lying counties of Lincolnshire and Nottinghamshire, this area is neatly bisected by a long ridge of limestone hills running northwards from east Leicestershire along the line of Lincoln Edge to the Humber. Throughout the eastern half of Leicestershire and all along that line, which is the northern extension of the great limestone belt that stretches from Dorset to Yorkshire, houses are built of stone—stone moreover of a very high quality, for the oolitic limestones of east Leicestershire and south Lincolnshire have for centuries been used all over the country and still produce to-day some of the most popular and reliable limestones after Portland stone itself.

To the east of the limestone ridge, and separated from it by the wide clay valley of the rivers Witham and Ancholme, lie the chalk Wolds and, beyond them again, the coastal marshes. To the west of the limestone ridge is the broad fenny valley of the Trent, which flows due north through Triassic marls and sandstones before joining the Ouse in an expanse of reed beds and tidal flats to form the Humber.

Geologically, the formation of the area is simple. The grain of the country runs purposefully north and south in more or less parallel bands of rock, the more resistant strata of chalk and oolite forming quite steep west-facing scarps along the line of the Wolds and Lincoln Edge. Sands and clays have been deposited over the basic strata of much of the region during the Ice Age and

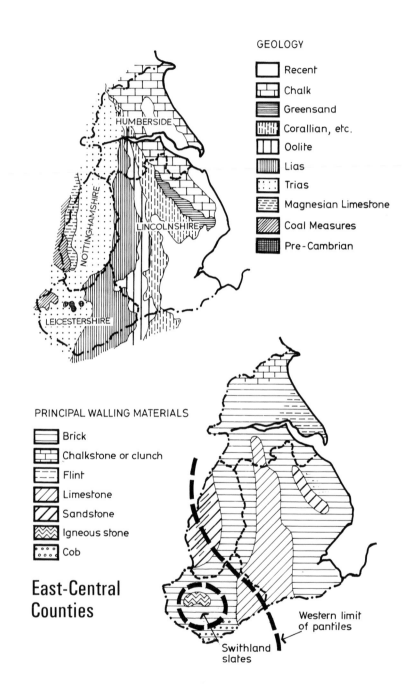

GEOLOGY

- Recent
- Chalk
- Greensand
- Corallian, etc.
- Oolite
- Lias
- Trias
- Magnesian Limestone
- Coal Measures
- Pre-Cambrian

HUMBERSIDE

NOTTINGHAMSHIRE

LINCOLNSHIRE

LEICESTERSHIRE

PRINCIPAL WALLING MATERIALS

- Brick
- Chalkstone or clunch
- Flint
- Limestone
- Sandstone
- Igneous stone
- Cob

East-Central Counties

Western limit of pantiles

Swithland slates

provide ample material for brickmaking almost everywhere except on the bare tops of the chalk and limestone hills.

Because of the regular pattern of the geology, the long journey going with the grain of the country from south to north will take the traveller along a constant formation, where the appearance of the land and style of building hardly changes from Leicestershire to the Humber. By contrast, the shorter east–west journey across the grain is one of great variety in which the landscape changes every few miles with the changing geology. The change in building styles from east to west is however not so marked as that of the landscape, except for the total change from brick to limestone in the centre, for the brick buildings of marsh, wolds, fens and valley have many features in common. Even the buildings of the far west, where the land rises to the magnesian limestone of the county boundary, are so influenced by the coalfields and the associated industrial developments of the nineteenth and twentieth centuries in that area that brick is used almost universally, whatever the rocks beneath have to offer; here the cottage rows of local pink sandstones and limestones, although pleasant enough with their modest proportions and timber lintels, are very much in the minority.

The main unifying feature of the buildings of Lincolnshire and Nottinghamshire is the pantiled roof. Introduced into all the East Coast ports from the Netherlands in the seventeenth century, the pantiles were shipped up-river into the interior and, as in south-west England, their distribution is well defined and is limited by the navigability of the inland waterways of the seventeenth, eighteenth and nineteenth centuries. From Barton-on-Humber, where some of the first English pantiles were made, the tiles were shipped up the Humber and Trent or coastwise to any of the little East Coast ports.

The pantiles of this region differ from those of East Anglia only in their colour, which here is seldom buff, nearly always red—a strong red in the south of the region, a bright, pale red in the centre and a darker, browner red in the north. The almost universal profile of the pantiles is the double curve or S-shape, which gives the roof a pronounced regularly furrowed appearance. Far less frequently seen is the small-scale double-S, which gives a much more even overall ripple to the roof.

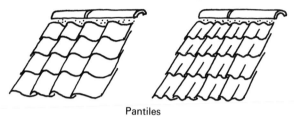

Pantiles

Tiles are often jointed with mortar, particularly in the older buildings; this makes for a slightly softer texture, since the jointing eliminates the sharp shadows between the tiles and modifies the colour, as pointing does in brickwork. When pantiles are stripped from cottages for repair or demolition, an underlying layer of hay or straw is sometimes seen, acting as an efficient insulation. No doubt such techniques were introduced at the time when the tiles were substituted for thatch. Tiles, for all their advantages of permanence and incombustibility, must have been desperately uncomfortable compared with cosy thatch—warm in winter, cool in summer.

The only part of the region where pantiles are quite unknown is in the western half of Leicestershire, where roofs are of slate or plain tiles. Everywhere else in the region they are practically universal, except that in the extreme eastern corner of Leicestershire the use of stone slates has spread across the Welland from Collyweston in Northamptonshire, and here both stone and pantiled roofs can be seen together.

Pantiled cottages

80

81

82

83

EAST-CENTRAL COUNTIES

80 Bruntingthorpe, LEICESTERSHIRE. Graded Swithland slates on a red-brick farmhouse (*page 115*)

81 Wildsworth, LINCOLNSHIRE. Cottages in brown bricks and pantiles beside the Trent (*page 114*)

82 Aby, LINCOLNSHIRE. A single-storey fenland cottage (*page 120*)

83 Bottesford, LEICESTERSHIRE. A large farmhouse in the Nottinghamshire red-brick tradition (*page 115*)

84

85

86

87

EAST-CENTRAL COUNTIES

84 Knossington, LEICESTERSHIRE. A tall eighteenth-century stone inn with a pronounced pattern of timber lintels (*page 118*)

85 Caldecott, LEICESTERSHIRE. A fine marlstone house in the Northamptonshire tradition, roofed in stone slates from Collyweston (*page 117*)

86 Castle Bytham, LINCOLNSHIRE. Bright-red pantiles and pale limestone (*page 117*)

87 Welby, LINCOLNSHIRE. Sliding 'Yorkshire' windows in a cottage of Lincolnshire limestone (*pages 113 & 134*)

88

89

90

NORTH-CENTRAL COUNTIES

88 Selside, Ribblesdale, NORTH YORKSHIRE. A Dales farm with its protecting sycamores (*page 130*)

89 Gargrave, NORTH YORKSHIRE. This fine seventeenth-century stone-roofed farmhouse has red stone quoins and projecting kneelers (*pages 126 & 127*)

90 Yockenthwaite in Langstrothdale, NORTH YORKSHIRE. A grey Mountain Limestone farm beside the Upper Wharf (*page 128*)

91

92

93

94

NORTH-CENTRAL COUNTIES

91 Farndale, NORTH YORKSHIRE. Red pantiles and warm grey stones in the North Yorkshire Moors (*page 135*)

92 Hovingham, NORTH YORKSHIRE. The generous proportions of the valley country (*page 133*)

93 Hathersage, DERBYSHIRE. Robust gritstone masonry (*page 128*)

94 Haworth, WEST YORKSHIRE. Sandstone cottages with gritstone window surrounds and stone-tiled roofs in the industrial Pennines (*page 126*)

The effect of the pantiled roofs on the character of the buildings can hardly be over-emphasised. They are large in scale, dominant in colour and, because of the comparative difficulty of cutting and manipulation, make a very simple roof shape. Thus, everywhere there are plain, uncomplicated gabled roofs, usually bright red, with the regular, large-scale rhythm of the tile ribs running down the slope. Dormers are few and simple and, as in East Anglia, of the 'cat-slide' shape, only gabled where tiles have replaced earlier thatch or where a Victorian builder has been rich enough to ignore the economic demands of his material and to indulge in a contrived roof shape.

On older buildings previously thatched, pitches can be steep, but normally pantiled roofs are about 40° pitch. Only the older or grander houses have parapets to their gables; the later and simpler buildings have none.

Pantiles are used on brick and stone buildings and impart a simplicity of form to both. Their warmth of colour and texture makes a perfect complement to the pale grey limestone of south Lincolnshire [87] (if a somewhat less happy combination with the yellow stone further north in the county) and seems to help the rather ordinary brick buildings of the lowland areas to achieve their distinctive appearance.

The brickwork of the northern Trent valley is clearly influenced by its Dutch ancestry. The bricks themselves are small, often only $2\frac{1}{4}$ in (57 mm) thick, and of a dark-brown, sometimes blackish appearance. The effect is pleasing and the houses fit well into their landscape of wide, flat fields, river levees and rows of trees, with the ever-present hills and woods not far away. The typical building of the area is of two storeys,

Corbelled eaves

eighteenth- or nineteenth-century, simple and rather elegant, relying on dark brickwork and a well proportioned arrangement of doors and windows for its appeal [81]. A corbelled dentil course of alternately projecting and recessed header bricks is a universal detail beneath the eaves, while gables are frequently finished, especially in the older houses, with brickwork verges or parapets built so that the coping bricks are at right angles to the slope. The resulting triangles of 'tumbled' brickwork are an important feature of the brick buildings of the eastern and northern parts of the region and can be seen in some parts of East Anglia as well. The technique originated in the Netherlands, as did the fashion for curved Dutch gable parapets, which can occasionally be seen on the ends of the larger houses in the Trent valley below Gainsborough, where Flemish influence is most felt. Windows and doors in all these buildings have curved segmental brick arches. (The often seen flat arch with the fan-shaped arrangement of bricks is a Georgian fashion, common to the whole of Britain in the eighteenth and nineteenth centuries, and is not a feature of local vernacular architecture.) Such houses as these are at their most striking when seen along the side of a dyke, beside the slow brown waters of the Trent or across the broad gleaming reaches of the Humber.

Tumbled brickwork

Further south between Gainsborough and Newark the brickwork is often bright-red, which, with the bright red pantiles of the area, gives a startling but not at all unpleasant appearance to the buildings. The consistently good brickwork, often a full red, of the fine, large Nottinghamshire farmhouses is also striking [83].

Large Nottinghamshire farmhouse

By contrast, the red-brick buildings of west and south Leicestershire and in the Charnwood Forest area are much more modest and would be quite unremarkable if it were not for their roofs, which on many eighteenth- and nineteenth-century buildings are of local Swithland slates. These are large and rough, but true slates, usually laid to a low pitch of about 30°, graded from large slates at the eaves to smaller ones at the ridge (nineteenth-century Welsh slates are never graded but are the same size from eaves to ridge), with a splendid variation of colour ranging from dark blue-greens to smokey greys [80]. They make a rugged roof that lends character to many otherwise rather uninteresting buildings.

Charnwood Forest itself is an isolated outcrop, quite out of its geological context in this part of England, of very hard and ancient pre-Cambrian rocks, in association with which there are local outcrops of pink granite north of Leicester at Mountsorrel and slates which have been quarried for a long time in the area of Swithland and nearby. The Forest is a small upland area of steep green fields and brackeny hills crowned with dark, rocky tors. The area adjoins the Staffordshire coalfield on the west and is rather built up as a consequence, but it is notably prettier and more rural along its northern edge, where the land descends to the valley of the Trent. Walling in the older buildings is of the rough dark greenish stone of the tors or of the even rougher pink granite boulders to the north of the Forest. The majority of buildings however are of red brick or are rendered or white-washed.

South of Leicester, the countryside quickly frees itself from the influence of the coalfields. Here the Triassic marls and clays produce a pastoral, rolling landscape, green and rural, with wide, grassy verges on either side of the long, straight eighteenth-century lanes. Field boundaries are beautifully kept, immensely broad, low hawthorn hedges, a notable feature of the landscape and entirely appropriate to a hunting county. The sudden appearance of rocky outcrops in this gentle scene is something of a shock. In a small area of south-west Leicestershire, from Stoney Stanton to Enderby, dark, ancient igneous rocks protrude through the soft Triassic fields to make their jagged mark against the sky and to lend the buildings and garden walls in their immediate vicinity an unexpectedly stern and sombre appearance among the generally brick buildings round about.

This area was once famous for its cob buildings, but, although occasional examples can be found, there are too few remaining to have any very important effect on the character of the country as we see it to-day.

The eastern half of Leicestershire lies on the brown Liassic limestone, except for the extreme eastern tip of the county, which is on the oolite. Much of the area is overlain with deposits of sands and clays which supported dense forests until these were cleared for agriculture during the Middle Ages. Buildings are of brick, and the character does not change very much until nearly on the banks of the Welland, the boundary of Northamptonshire, where villages like Slawton and Great Easton are built of the yellowy-brown marlstone, often striped with grey limestone bands from the oolite nearby.

The Welland valley is wide and open, although on a small and intimate scale, and is beautifully served by its buildings and its hills. Steep-sided on the south and gently undulating on the north, it presents as pretty a picture of English landscape as it would be possible to find anywhere.

From here north-eastwards towards what used to be Rutland the buildings are all of limestone. The powerful stylistic influence of the Northamptonshire vernacular is everywhere to be seen [85]: steep-pitched roofs of Collyweston slates, parapetted gables, gabled bay windows, stone mullions and a mixture of marlstone and oolite in walling—brown walls with grey quoins and dressings or walling in alternate stripes of brown and grey—all charmingly done but all on a slightly smaller scale than in Northamptonshire.

Around Stamford lie the rich limestone quarries of Ketton, Barnack and, perhaps best known, Clipsham. Further north towards Lincoln, in a gap in the narrow limestone ridge, lies Ancaster, another famous quarry name. These quarries, and others whose names may be less well known, provided freestones and ragstones that were transported all over England in the Middle Ages and after, for many of our great churches and cathedrals. Locally, the stone is of course the basis of the vernacular. Houses are pale grey or whiteish, built with carefully dressed, well-coursed blocks of stone, and, because of the wealth created by the quarries, the wool trade and the sheep-rearing, are on a larger scale and a good deal better built than the brick buildings further west [86].

Here in the limestone hills mullioned windows do not have the medieval hooded drip-stone above them, as in the Cotswolds and most of Northamptonshire, but a simple, classical-style string-mould without a turn-down at the ends. As the moulding has no undercut drip to throw off the water, its presence, although practically universal in the older and richer houses, can only be ascribed to decoration and not to function. But mouldings and stone mullions are by no means the norm for

stone buildings in this region, as they are in the limestone areas
of Gloucestershire and much of Northamptonshire. Here stone
buildings of the eighteenth and nineteenth centuries nearly all
have wooden lintels. These are of oak, are long and thin, are
always painted the same colour as the windows and, projecting
widely beyond the sides of the windows, make a distinctive
pattern on the face of the buildings [84].

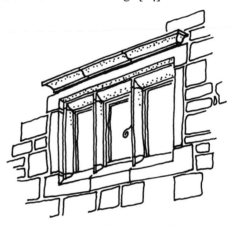

A Leicestershire stone window

Further away from Collyweston, stone slates become less
common, until in Clipsham many of the simpler buildings have
red pantiled roofs, and farther away still, in Castle Bytham, only
the grander houses have stone ones.

The villages of the Lincoln Edge, mostly sited below the scarp
along the line of springs, are exclusively roofed in red pantiles.
The stone here is cream-coloured and gets progressively darker
in tone and more rubbly northwards towards Lincoln. With the
warmer tone and less well dressed stone, the classical element of
the pale grey Rutland-type house is lost, yet these villages glow
pleasantly enough, with red roofs and cream walls. North of
Lincoln, where the stone gets even more rubbly and assumes a
darker biscuit colour, the effect of the red pantiles is less pleasant,
and the red-brick quoins and window surrounds that are

necessary because of the rough quality of the stone do little to improve the appearance of the buildings.

West of the Edge lies the undulating plain of the Lias, which rises northwards to the ironstone ridge of hills where Scunthorpe and its ironworks are busily scooping away the landscape.

Eastwards across the valley lie the Wolds, chalk hills with smooth contours, in parts overlain with boulder clay. Here on the open hills, farms are isolated and nearly all of the nineteenth century. Beneath the Wolds and along their western boundary lies a strip of Greensand which becomes wider towards the south until the southern extremity of the Wolds is almost entirely made of Greensand hills. Spilsby sandstone, although often referred to, is not much in evidence in the surrounding villages, but further north, along the edge of the Wolds, lie Tealby and adjacent villages, where a charming buff sandstone from the Greensand is used to great effect.

Surrounding the Wolds and extending far southwards towards the Norfolk border lie the marshes and the fens.

There are no dramatic islands in the Lincolnshire fens comparable with the Isle of Ely, nor is any of the land actually below sea-level, but otherwise the area's history and appearance are similar to those of the Cambridgeshire and Norfolk fenlands.

The land lies level under its huge canopy of sky, with no break from the wind other than the short rows of trees planted to protect the crops, and no break for the eye but the church spires that mark the parishes and the electricity pylons that stalk across the plain in endless rows. Bright fields of tulips, cream and pink, yellow, white and red in stripes of colour, relieve the monotony and the little houses along the roads are cheerful in brick or whitewash. These are usually Victorian in style, with Welsh slate roofs.

As in Cambridgeshire, the silt fens nearer the coast were the more easily drained and so were developed earlier. Brought into cultivation by generations of labour, by the thirteenth century the silt fens were mostly in pasture for sheep owned by the monasteries. It is here that the older houses and villages are found. Further inland the peat fens were drained later and, because the black soil of the peat fen shrinks and makes poor and difficult foundations, there are few villages in the area. The red soil of the silt fens is however relatively stable and supports such towns as Boston and Spalding. It is along the quays of these old towns that the vernacular of the fenlands is at its most striking. Along the muddy tidal creeks, the wharfs and warehouses might have been taken straight from the Hanseatic ports or from the Netherlands. Tall, many-windowed, with slate or pantiled roofs, these huge brown buildings reflect the prosperity enjoyed by such towns from the Middle Ages until the eighteenth century, although by the latter date their full prosperity lay already in the past.

Among the fields of the red silt fens are isolated farms and cottages of some antiquity. The cottages are small and low and are all to a pattern; they are usually of the eighteenth century, often with a storey in the roof which sweeps down low at the back. Sometimes whitewashed, invariably pantiled, these simple brick buildings seem to crouch under the weight of wind and sky [82].

A Lincolnshire fen cottage

The salt marshes, which lie between the Wolds and the sea beyond, where the steep, east-facing side of the chalk hills proclaims an ancient sea cliff, were drained at much the same time as the peat fens, and here the population is similarly scanty. Even so, occasional large old farmhouses are to be seen, as at Saltfleetby All Saints, built in soft, warm red brick, with tumbled gables and warm red pantiles, lichen-covered and hoary. In such roofs as these the form of the dormer windows, the steep pitch and the height of the gable parapets show that the pantiles have supplanted earlier thatch.

Lincolnshire is far the largest county in the region and by far the largest part of Lincolnshire is taken up by marshlands and fens. It is not therefore inappropriate to leave the region with a memory of fenlands, for there will be nothing comparable to these strange, man-made landscapes in the remaining chapters.

An early manor farmhouse (Lincolnshire)

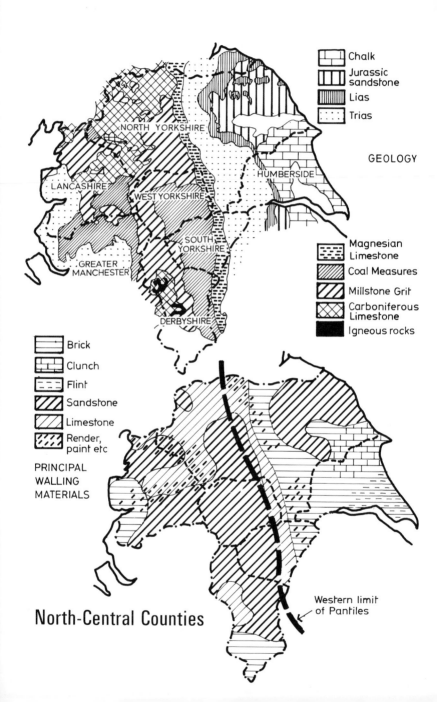

GEOLOGY

Chalk
Jurassic sandstone
Lias
Trias

NORTH YORKSHIRE

LANCASHIRE

WEST YORKSHIRE

HUMBERSIDE

SOUTH YORKSHIRE

GREATER MANCHESTER

DERBYSHIRE

Magnesian Limestone
Coal Measures
Millstone Grit
Carboniferous Limestone
Igneous rocks

Brick
Clunch
Flint
Sandstone
Limestone
Render, paint etc

PRINCIPAL WALLING MATERIALS

Western limit of Pantiles

North-Central Counties

9. North-Central Counties
Derbyshire, Yorkshire and Lancashire
The Pennine Heartland and its Neighbours

The major theme of the whole region is one of stern stone buildings in an upland setting. Simple and direct building techniques and magnificent materials have created a vernacular style whose influence is dominant in Northern England.

The hilly Pennine range, which comprises more than half the area of the region, is flanked by the small lowland area of the Lancashire plain on the west and by a much larger and more varied area on the east. The North Yorkshire moors fall in the latter area and are upland in character, but all the remainder is lowland, including the Vale of York and the chalk Wolds of north Humberside. The buildings of the lowlands have their own charm and character, but pride of place must go to the stone farms and cottages of the Pennine moors and valleys.

Once again, the geology of the region dictates the appearance of its buildings, but here in a particularly dramatic and striking manner. The difference between the dark stones of the Pennine moorlands and the pale limestones of the Dales, between the brick and pantiles of the Yorkshire plain and the heavy stone roofs and solid stone walls of the hills, is as apparent as the differences in landscape and vegetation.

The southern half of the Pennine range is mainly composed of Millstone (or Moorstone) Grit, as uncompromising a rock as its names imply, hard, coarse and massive enough for the manufacture of millstones. (Some idea of the scale on which these were produced may be gained from the abandoned quarry under Millstone Edge a few miles outside Sheffield. Here hundreds and hundreds of millstones lie in all shapes and sizes and in all stages of manufacture, some cut but not rounded, some with the central hole formed and some without. There they lie in stacks and swathes, spilling down the lonely hillside, half smothered in bracken, fern and moss, a veritable graveyard of rural industry, abandoned in full production as though struck down by some natural catastrophe instead of mere economic decline.)

This hard and rugged stone varies when quarried from a dark grey to a hard pale buff colour and only assumes its almost black appearance in areas of high atmospheric pollution. In the central moorlands of West Yorkshire and north Derbyshire, where the buildings have suffered nearly two hundred years of smoke from the huge industrial concentrations of the coalfields which lie on either side of the Pennines southwards from the latitude of Burnley and Bradford, the buildings are black—lonely and forbidding on the tops or clustered together round the mills in the valleys. It is Brontë country, and of all the varied landscapes of the region it is the one which grips the imagination most powerfully. The moors comprise high, bleak upland tracts of acid soil, supporting little more than coarse bents, heather, bilberry, sphagnum moss and cotton-grass. Below the moors in the deep valleys, the black stone field boundaries emphasise the brilliance of the green pastures where the many bright and busy streams used to turn the woollen mills in the eighteenth and early nineteenth centuries.

A Pennine farm

The whole of the Pennine range has from the Middle Ages been concerned with sheep-raising and the production of woollen cloth. The wool was spun and woven in the farms and cottages throughout much of the area until the invention of power-driven spinning machinery gave rise in the eighteenth century to the construction of water-powered mills in the valley bottoms. In West Yorkshire an enormous number of farmhouses and cottages built in the late seventeenth and eighteenth centuries were built with specially constructed workrooms for weaving, usually on an upper storey but sometimes on the ground floor as well. The rooms had to be well lit and weavers' windows were introduced. These are long rows of windows, as many as nine lights in a row, divided by gritstone or sandstone mullions. Very long rows are divided into groups by larger 'master' mullions. In this region window frames within their stone surrounds are always made of wood and nearly always painted white.

Weavers' windows (West Yorkshire)

After the introduction of machine spinning and the building of the early mills, much of the weaving was still done in the homesteads until, at the end of the eighteenth century, machine looms were introduced, which signalled the demise of the cottage industry, although weavers' windows were still being built well into the nineteenth century. Steam power, using coal from the developing coalfields, gradually replaced water power, so that to-day every little tree-choked valley sprouts its chimney-stack—frequently now disused, as steam has in its turn been supplanted by oil, gas and electricity.

The gritstone (or the sandstone from the coalfields, especially the famous York stone) of which the houses are built is easily cut when fresh from the quarry and can be had in large pieces ideally suited to making window and door surrounds, mullions and lintels [94]. Houses in these areas are usually made of large, regularly coursed rectangular stones, all much of a size, the joints between being paler than the blackened stones themselves.

Gritstone cottages (West Yorkshire)

Windows and doors are invariably surrounded with long stones forming jambs, lintels or sills; the technique of building door jambs with one or two long, thin vertical stones rather than building the jambs up with the walling masonry is peculiar to the later Pennine-type buildings and is a direct outcome of the availability of material in a convenient form. The shaped mullions and window surrounds, following the medieval tradition which persisted at least until the end of the seventeenth century, are replaced in later houses by simple square sections.

A particularly prominent feature of stone houses in the region is the kneeler, or stone bracket terminating the gable parapet at the eaves [89]. The kneeler serves as a visual termination to the

Seventeenth- and eighteenth-century stone mullions

sloping parapet stones and stops them looking as though they might slide off. Kneelers, often rather crude and exaggerated in form, do lend the houses one of their few decorative touches, albeit rather an aggressive one.

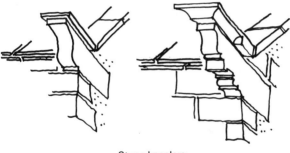

Stone kneelers

Roofs in the gritstone and sandstone areas are invariably of stone slabs. The stones, which split naturally to a surprisingly true surface, come from brownish sandstone strata in the rocks immediately beneath the gritstone (the Yoredale rocks) or from similar formations in the Coal Measures [89]. Often huge, sometimes gigantic, the stones are seldom rough and fit tightly together. Roofs are heavy and keep the water out well, so that for the most part roof pitches are low, around 30° or less. Eaves hardly overhang at all, gables (usually parapetted) are universal, and chimneys, constructed of the fewest possible slabs of utterly black stone, are situated at the ends of the roof. In the older and grander houses, the roof shape can be complex, with subsidiary roofs to projecting wings or two-storey porches running at right angles to the main ridge, but generally building forms are simple, to suit the large roofing stones. In eighteenth- and nineteenth-century houses, small stone brackets, widely spaced beneath the eaves, make a sort of cornice and form supports for the wooden gutters (now increasingly replaced with metal or plastic) which were usual in the more polite buildings.

Old farmhouse (North Yorkshire)

The buildings of the millstone grit areas of Derbyshire that surround the Dales and form the High Peak are similar in character to those of West Yorkshire [93, 97].

Beneath the Coal Measures and the Millstone Grit, and forming much of the Yorkshire Dales and of central Derbyshire, lies the Carboniferous or Mountain Limestone. This noble rock creates an entirely different landscape to the grit. Pale grey, almost lilac in certain lights, it creates a landscape of light, of pale bare rocks outcropping in cliffs, gorges and pavements, and it supports a large population of sheep on its pale green grassy slopes [90]. The lime-tolerant plants of the Mountain Limestone—scabious, orchis, campion and saxifrage—make a bright and cheerful contrast to the grander and darker tones of the heathers and bilberries of the grit. The difference between this landscape and that of the gritstone can be truly startling in the Derbyshire Dales, where it is possible to look from a bleak,

95

96

97

98

NORTH-CENTRAL COUNTIES

95 Grindleton, LANCASHIRE. Colour-washed rubbly stonework with stone surrounds to
square windows (*page 133*)

96 Barrowford, Nelson, LANCASHIRE. Many-mullioned windows and low-pitched stone
roofs (*pages 132 & 133*)

97 Sparrowpit, DERBYSHIRE. Sandstone cottages in the Peak District (*page 128*)

98 Knowle Green, LANCASHIRE. The fierce gaiety of the pointing on this gritstone inn is
typical of Lancashire (*page 133*)

99

100

101

102

NORTHERN ENGLAND

99 Stonethwaite, Borrowdale, CUMBRIA. A fine Lakeland farmhouse. The garden wall is of cobbles from the stream (*pages 141, 142 & 143*)

100 Middle Fell Farm, Langdale, CUMBRIA. The long roof of this Lakeland farm covers whitewashed house and plain stone byre (*page 139*)

101 Elterwater, CUMBRIA. Cottage made of green slate quarry waste (*page 141*)

102 Hartsop, CUMBRIA. A thick circular chimney on an old farmhouse (*page 142*)

103

104

105

106

NORTHERN ENGLAND

103 Cleator Moor, CUMBRIA. Polychrome paintwork and render in the Cumbrian coalfield (*page 144*)
104 Gosforth, CUMBRIA. Green slate roofs on rendered cottages (*page 144*)
105 Long Marton, Vale of Eden, CUMBRIA. Black-painted window surrounds set off the Red Sandstone walls (*pages 144 & 145*)
106 Shap, CUMBRIA. Heavy, rough granite and colour-wash (*page 141*)

107

108

109

110

NORTHERN ENGLAND

107 Old Mousen, Belford, NORTHUMBERLAND. Single-storey row of estate stone cottages (*pages 147 & 148*)

108 Near Housesteads, NORTHUMBERLAND. Stone farm on the Roman Wall (*page 146*)

109 Blanchland, NORTHUMBERLAND. A splendid example of Pennine building in stone (*page 146*)

110 Near Newbiggin, DURHAM. One of the small isolated farmhouses in Upper Teesdale (*page 146*)

dark gritstone moorland directly down into a bright limestone dale hundreds of feet below.

In the Derbyshire Dales the landscape is dramatic, restless and abrupt. Hills are steep and high, valleys are narrow, deep and often wooded, their sides precipitous. Villages are of necessity on the uplands. Dark igneous rocks intrude in the limestone hills and these (called toadstones when used in buildings) and the limestone itself are quarried on a huge scale for road metalling and lime. Lead was mined in the hills for centuries; now fluorspar is mined. The hills have a worked-over look that lends the countryside a mildly disreputable air, but for all that the streams are as limpid, the wild flowers are as vivid and the pale stone is as beautiful as anywhere in England.

Here all houses are built of the pale Mountain Limestone, mostly of roughly coursed rubble occasionally spotted with black toadstones and with corner-stones and surrounds to doors and windows of grit, slightly darker or yellower than the walls. Some of the Derbyshire limestones are a little softer, and in these districts houses have squared and neatly coursed walling with limestone lintels and corner-stones, all of the same whiteish-grey.

Over a large part of south Derbyshire, as in the adjacent area of east Staffordshire, roofs are of dark, purply-blue plain tiles. Their striking dark shade, slightly shiny, is a distinctive feature of the brick buildings in the lowland areas south of the hills and contrasts splendidly with the pale limestone walling and the pale tones of the limestone country further to the north [75]. The tiles come from the area of Stoke-on-Trent and are of a similar clay to that from which the famous 'Staffordshire Blues' are made, although the tiles are notably more purple than those celebrated engineering bricks. Roof pitches for the plain tiles are of about 40° to 45°, rather lower than is usual in south-east England where the red, slightly irregular and hump-backed plain tiles need a steeper slope.

The limestone country of the Yorkshire Dales, although geologically similar, is on far larger and more serene a scale. Farmed for centuries, smoothed by the Ice Age, well watered, self-sufficient and prosperous, the Yorkshire Dale country is one of the few areas in the world where man and nature have achieved what seems a lasting harmony. The wide, smooth valleys and the classical hill-forms provide a setting for pale-grey buildings of great simplicity and nobility of proportion.

In some dales the buildings cluster together in close-knit grey villages, in others isolated farmsteads are regularly spaced out down the valley, each with its cluster of roofs and its sycamore trees, much as the independent Norse settlers laid out their lodges in the Dark Ages [88].

The pattern of farms and farm buildings varies according to locality and date throughout the Dales. Many of the older farms are attached to their byres and barns under one long roof—the classical long-house pattern—but later farms tended to have separate field barns scattered along the hillsides for winter shelter and hay storage. These barns are called 'laithes'. There are several patterns but the most striking have a big porch for driving in the hay-wains to shelter from the frequent sudden rainstorms. The field barns above Malham are a famous and notable group that gives style and character to the whole neighbourhood. Again, especially further south, the later farms may have their laithes attached to the houses, with huge, arched openings for the wagons.

A farmhouse with laithe attached (West Yorkshire)

All these buildings have brown stone-slated roofs, quarried from the Yoredale series of rocks. These lie immediately above the Limestone and are formed of alternate layers of hard and soft rock; they make terraces on the hillsides and steps in the valley bottoms over which the rivers plunge in cascades and waterfalls. Ash trees are everywhere along the stream sides, every farmhouse has its sycamores and everywhere are the sheep.

In the Dales the fields are comparatively small and all are bounded by stone walls. These pale grey field walls are an important feature of the limestone country and define with their sweeping parallel curves the shape of the land on which they are built.

The Arcadian effect of the landscape is heightened by the form of the buildings, which have low-pitched roofs and a direct, simple walling technique of projecting 'through' stones used almost universally in the outbuildings and barns and sometimes in the houses too. These are special long bonding-stones which run through the wall so as to bind the inner and outer stones together, but left projecting quite a long way in rough broken courses around the buildings, which saves cutting the stones to the width of the wall. The effect is reminiscent of Alpine or even Italian farm buildings.

As in the gritstone country, seventeenth-century buildings abound, the older ones with very small windows and many with strange and elaborately carved door lintels. The patterns for these are traditional and varied but seem to follow no recognisable canon of design. They incorporate the date and often the

Carved door lintel (West Yorkshire)

initials of the owner and his wife. Here the air is clean, so the sandstone only goes black on the chimney-stacks, the dressings elsewhere staying grey, buff or pale brown.

Beyond the Pennines to the west lie the Forest of Bowland, the Pendle Hills, the valley of the Ribble and the Lancashire coalfields. Over all this varied hilly area buildings have the same basic Pennine characteristics of simplicity and sturdiness, grim and uncompromising on the Grit, which here is somewhat yellower than in Yorkshire, mellower on the Limestone, dark and sometimes dilapidated on the Coal Measures. In the Trough of Bowland, iron-stained boulders from the rivers are often roughly dressed and used as slightly rounded walling stones.

In the coalmining districts the stone is browner and noticeably more horizontally stratified, so that pieces of stone in the walls are long and thin, giving quite a different appearance to the houses [96]. In the Pendle Hills and the Ribble valley houses are generally of limestone, which further west and towards Morecambe Bay goes quite pink and even red in colour.

But the main feature of all the lowland Lancashire houses (often including those in the flat coastal plain, where the Pennine character gives place to a brick vernacular of no great individuality) is the use of applied or finishing materials. External render (plasterwork made with grit, sand and cement or lime), whitewash, colour-wash and paintwork are all used to great effect

Lancashire rendering and paint

[95]. Nowhere is paint used so stylishly as in Lancashire. The colours applied to the wide rendered window and door surrounds are subtle and usually dark, ranging from black through greys and mid-browns to reduced dark greens chosen to contrast, often violently, with white- or yellow-painted windows and doors or with the gentler natural colours of the render derived from the greys, pinks and buffs of the sands and gravels of which it is made. The effect is to give the Lancashire buildings a sort of fierce, bright gaiety, totally at variance with the dreamy buildings of the Dales and the sombre buildings of the moors. Rendered walls with painted corner-stones and window surrounds, whether of stone or simulated in render; black stone walls with joints picked out in white [98]; ancient stone buildings with black-painted stone mullions and window surrounds and white window frames—all are characteristic of the area.

In the hilly districts roofs are of brown stone slabs, the Rossendale flags from the Coal Measures south of Burnley being typical [96].

Most development in the coalmining districts is of the late eighteenth and nineteenth centuries; consequently windows are squarish and relatively large, and many of the houses are built in terraced rows. Brick clays are abundant here, as in other

Painted stone surrounds (Lancashire)

coalmining districts, and the famous engineering bricks from Accrington, hard, dark red and heavy, give many Victorian buildings their fine, sombre appearance.

Across to the east on the other side of the Pennines lies the Vale of York. Here the country is oriented towards the North Sea, as is made evident by the universal red pantiled roofs. This is a complete break with the Pennine tradition. The architecture of the Vale is reminiscent of that of Lincolnshire and Humberside, but shows a greater prosperity in the larger and more solidly built houses that accords well with the rich farming country, flat, well watered and rather dull. These houses are straightforward eighteenth-century brick or stone two-storeyed buildings with uncomplicated red pantiled roofs [92]. Where rooms are in the roof space, the dormer windows are roofed, as in Lincolnshire, with sloping cat-slides. The bricks are a handsome browny-red, less brindled than further south beyond the Humber, and the stone varies between a pale buttery cream colour on the west of the Vale (where the Magnesian Limestone outcrops in a narrow north–south band) and a browny-yellow stone on the east (where the Lias forms the western slopes of the Hambleton Hills). But, apart from its eastern and western margins, the Vale is an area of mainly brick buildings. Here, and generally in the south and east of the region, windows in eighteenth- and nineteenth-century farms and cottages are very often of the horizontally sliding sort. This 'Yorkshire sliding window' is also seen further south in Humberside and Lincolnshire and occasionally elsewhere in England, but its home is undoubtedly in Yorkshire [87].

The North Yorkshire Moors are an upland region of yellow and grey sandstones from the Jurassic series (an unusual stone in England). The rock produces a gloomy upland plateau, covered in a very dark growth of heather, intersected by deep, steep and very pretty grassy valleys. The farms and villages, mostly developed in the eighteenth century, are all in the valleys, and the houses, built of the yellow-grey stone with bright red pantiled roofs, are some of the prettiest in Yorkshire. Isolated farmhouses—neatly spaced out along the length of valleys, like Farndale—are typically of two storeys, with a byre attached to

Farmhouse, North Yorkshire Moors

one end, considerably lower than the house, so that the pantiled roof is discontinuous [91]. The barns are built separately from the houses, so a completely different picture is presented to that of the Pennine farms. Here too the colour scheme of buffs, yellows and reds, against their background of green grass and trees beneath the looming moorland tops, is a total change from Pennine dales and moors.

At the coast, where the steep sandstone and Lias cliffs fall hundreds of feet to the North Sea, every little inlet is crowded

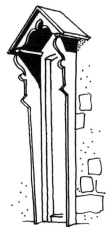

Doorway, Robin Hood's Bay (North Yorkshire)

with the red pantiled roofs of the fishermen's houses as they huddle down the steep slopes to the quayside. Here walls are whitewashed or left in unpainted stone, and alleyways are narrow, steep and paved in sandstone slabs and cobbles. Front doors give straight onto the alleyways and are furnished with quirky little wooden porches, each cut to a slightly different pattern, with a circumflex roof like a shallow decorative sentry-box.

On the south edge of the Moors and adjacent to the Vale of Pickering is a line of villages where the moorland's yellowish rock gives way to a very much whiter stone. This stone is used in the Howardian Hills, across the western end of the Vale, where houses are again of simple eighteenth-century design.

Across the Vale, flat-bottomed as befits the bed of an ancient glacial lake, lie the chalk Wolds, where, apart from some older cottages built in blocks of white clunch from the Lower Chalk, farms and cottages are of brick and are of comparatively recent date. Pantiled roofs are still universal, but flint buildings are not typical of these chalklands as they are in the south of England.

We have seen how the style of building in the Vale of York is similar to that of adjacent Lincolnshire and thus transgresses a rather arbitrarily drawn regional boundary. This is very much the case with the region discussed in the next chapter, where the Pennine style of building covers the remaining central uplands at least as far as the South Tyne. However, this is not a major building type in the next region as a whole, which is dominated by the powerful Cumbrian vernacular and by the more recessive style of Northumberland.

Field barns, Yorkshire dales

10. Northern England
Cumbria, Northumberland and Durham
Lakeland and the Border

Cumbria, Northumberland and Durham together form the true North of England. There is however no doubt that the romantic associations of Lakeland, its wild and rugged scenery and the highly characteristic buildings to which its geology has given rise, combine to make Cumbria, from our point of view, by far the most important of the three.

The Lake District hills are made up of very hard ancient, mineral-bearing slatey rocks from the Silurian and Ordovician series, together with large areas of rock of volcanic origin, which combine to form the dome-like structure of the district, whose deep and often narrow valleys hold the lakes themselves.

Lakeland is an area of great contrasts—of high colouring in shades of purple and bright green, of violent relief with crags and precipices, and of dark woods and bright water. Valleys radiate from the central mass of the hills, and roads, joining valley to valley, are steep, tortuous, and sometimes non-existent. In spite of this, apart from minor variations of technique between one valley and the next, all the more important aspects of building style are consistent throughout the area.

The traditional buildings of the Lake District are all built of rocks, mostly slatey. Their character is somewhat severe, but when compared with the simpler buildings of the Pennines they have such a sombre depth of colour and richness of texture in their masonry and exhibit such unusual architectural features as to border on the exotic. The Victorians evidently tried to capture some of this quality in their buildings and developed many of the more accessible valleys, with their villa residences, hotels and

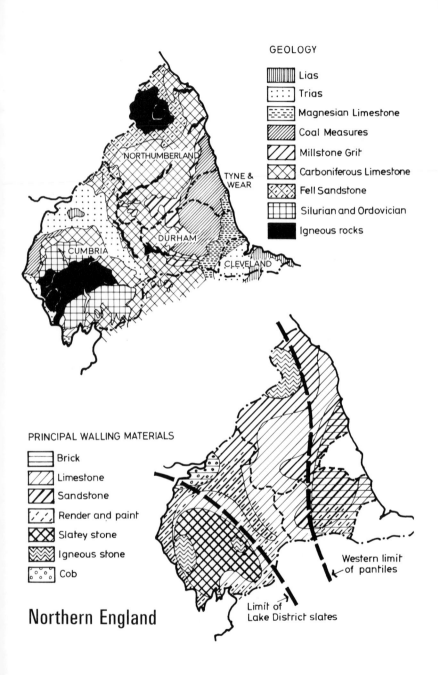

GEOLOGY

Lias
Trias
Magnesian Limestone
Coal Measures
Millstone Grit
Carboniferous Limestone
Fell Sandstone
Silurian and Ordovician
Igneous rocks

NORTHUMBERLAND

TYNE & WEAR

DURHAM

CUMBRIA

CLEVELAND

PRINCIPAL WALLING MATERIALS

Brick
Limestone
Sandstone
Render and paint
Slatey stone
Igneous stone
Cob

Western limit of pantiles

Limit of Lake District slates

Northern England

cottages, in a style they considered appropriate to a lakeside environment and mountainous background. The result is a wealth of overhanging eaves and verges, shutters, verandahs, turrets and complicated slate roofs, a style that in fact, whatever the intention, creates an almost total discord with the vernacular of the region.

The older Lakeland buildings are nearly all farmhouses; there are few cottages other than the not infrequent eighteenth- and nineteenth-century rows of workmen's cottages near the slate quarries or old lead mines. Farms are grouped in communities, as at Troutbeck or Hartsop, or are strung out one at a time along the floors of valleys, such as Great Langdale. The farmhouses themselves are most often whitewashed, the outbuildings being nearly always left in dark unpainted stone.

A Lakeland farm (Cumbria)

The traditional form for a Lakeland farm is that of a long-house, with house, byre and barn all joined together under one continuous roof [100]. Later improvements and additions in the wealthier houses may obscure this original pattern, and a variation on the long-house tradition is that sometimes the barn is built taller than the whitewashed house alongside. A shelf-like shed roof, called a 'pentice', is often provided above the barn and byre doorways to provide shelter immediately in front of the building, while doorways and windows in the outbuildings are

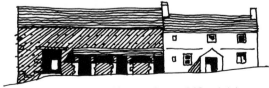

A barn with a pentice roof (Cumbria)

frequently surrounded in roughly applied whitewash, done partly for cleanliness and partly to make movement easier after dark, for the deep tones of the stonework, on an overcast and moonless winter's night, will reflect no glimmer to distinguish door from wall.

The stonework of which these buildings are made is distinctive and remarkable. Slate or slatey rock splits into long, thin pieces and these are laid with the mortar kept back from the face of the wall, which makes for dark shadows between the stones. The stones themselves too are dark grey, grey-blue, purple or, in the north of the district, tawny-brown. The exception is the much prized green slate, which is a pale blue-green and has been widely known as a high-quality roofing slate all over England since the seventeenth century. Its use was further popularised by the late nineteenth- and early twentieth-century architects, Voysey and Lutyens, who used many features of Westmorland traditional building in the style of domestic architecture which they pioneered.

Slate stones used in walling are of two sorts: those roughly quarried or taken from the screes and stream beds, and those taken from the waste tips of slate quarries. The former have a certain softness and indeterminacy of outline, while the latter stones have a savage sharpness of profile—even, in later examples, showing on their weather face the marks of the quarrymen's circular saws.

Cumbrian slate lintels

Near the quarries, such as in Elterwater, green slate is used for lintels and corner-stones since it can be got in very large pieces. These are thin, split stones, laid edgeways up, and their huge green irregular shapes make a startling contrast with the narrow darker slates of the walls [101].

In the west of the district, granite boulders are used for walling. Dark grey-pink and very rounded in shape, they make quite a different wall to the generality of slate walling elsewhere. The boulders are wedged up one above the other, with intervening courses of thin slates or small stones which produce a noticeably striped appearance in the buildings. In the east of the hills the famous quarry of Shap produces large dressed blocks of granite which can be seen as lintels and quoins in the local cottages [106].

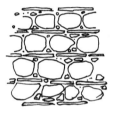

Boulders and slate

Roofs are of course of slate, pale grey and green, their colours subtly muted with grey lichens. The slates are rough, thick and beautifully laid in diminishing courses, from large, massive slates at the eaves to tiny pieces at the ridge [99]. Roofs do not overhang much and the pitch is generally low, about 30° to 35°.

An old Cumbrian farmhouse

Hips are unknown and gables are simple, usually unparapetted but occasionally stepped in the older seventeenth-century farms that aspired to some grandeur, the steps being finished with wide, flat slates. This device may have been adopted to stop the coping slates from sliding off if laid on the slope, perhaps to make it easier to get up the roof to the chimney. However that may be, the effect is not altogether happy, as it lends a certain fussiness to these otherwise fine buildings.

The chimneys are a distinctive and rather special feature of the early Lakeland farmhouses. In some of the older houses the chimneys terminate above the roof in round, slightly tapering stacks, built circular to avoid having to make corners out of stones, which were exceedingly difficult to cut to a reasonable rectangular shape [102]. The top of the flue, whether on a round or a square chimney, is protected from rain and snow by a pair of large slates leaning together, like the first stage of a card house.

Lakeland chimneys

End chimneys are frequently corbelled out from the top of the gable wall and have no chimney breast or supporting mass of masonry below, for the flue, leading up through the house, was made in the form of a lath and plaster hood, not built in masonry as elsewhere in England.

Although cottage rows have their doorways opening directly off the street, farmhouses very often have porches, deep and generous, with an arched opening, roofed in slates and always whitewashed inside [99].

Windows, apart from the very small chimney window on the ground floor next to the hearth, are large, squarish and usually with vertically sliding sashes, but some houses have an ingenious variation in which the top half pivots and the bottom half is fixed [99]. Sash windows may be later additions in older houses but nevertheless give a notable character to the Lakeland farms. Window heads are arched in rough stonework or bridged with simple lintels where stone could be got large enough.

Some of the more ancient farms have what is called a spinning gallery. This is a small outside covered verandah tucked under the slate roof and provided with an oak balustrade. The purpose of the gallery seems obscure. It may have been for airing the woollen yarn or for spinning, as the name implies, but if the latter, there was not much of a view for the spinner.

The pretty, tumbled, well wooded countryside that forms the southern foothills of the Lakeland massif is generally made of reddish carboniferous limestone. Here the houses are grey, rubble-walled and occasionally whitewashed. Further in towards the hills, the rock changes to the mountain type and there is more render and whitewash than bare stone. In Hawkshead the older buildings are almost universally white. This is one of the few old towns in the area and has an attractive, intimate medieval air of courtyards, overhanging upper storeys and rough grey roofs.

In comparison with those of the Lake District, the buildings of the surrounding low-lying areas of the Vale of Eden and the coastal plains are simple, straightforward and anything but exotic.

Coming down the mountainous valleys westwards into the narrow coastal plain, the sudden change from hard volcanic rocks to the soft New Red Sandstones of the Trias is very evident. The transition is neatly expressed in the Roman fortress where the Hardknott Pass opens into Eskdale, the walls being of rough grey volcanic rock from the hills, while the arch stones, which need to be precisely cut, are of soft red sandstone from the plain.

The buildings of the plain are generally later in date than those in the more prosperous of the mountain valleys; dark red sandstone blocks are the principal walling material and roofs are of rough grey-green slates from the Lakes. Occasionally larger farmhouses are rendered and whitewashed, leaving unpainted and in startling contrast only their dark red corner-stones and window dressings. More often, rendered houses have their stone dressings painted, for here, as in Lancashire, there is a great feeling for rendered surfaces and paint, generated no doubt by the porous and unsatisfactory nature of the unprotected sandstone [104].

Red sandstone and render (Cumbria)

Further north too, in the Cumbrian coalfield, render and paint are the rule. Throughout this part of the region paint is used with great spirit and virtuosity. In the long nineteenth-century rows of miners' cottages all the cottages are painted in bright contrasting colours, as though to defy with their polychrome any thought of depression, isolation or bad weather [103].

The Vale of Eden and the Solway Plain surround the Lake District on its eastern and northern flanks. This is a wide rich farmland, based on the pinkish Carboniferous Limestone and the soft, dark New Red Sandstone, both much overlain by glacial deposits. Sandstone buildings in this area are built with large squarish blocks of the dark red stone [105], and in transitional

111

112

113

WALES

111 Marionglas, ANGLESEY. A typical neat single-storey Anglesey farmhouse with a slurried roof (*page 162*)

112 Near Harlech, GWYNEDD. Hillside cottage built of the ancient Cambrian rocks of the Harlech Dome (*page 152*)

113 Maenaddwyn, ANGLESEY. The slurried roof is whitewashed as well as the rugged stone walls of this little post office (*pages 156 & 160*)

114

115

116

117

WALES

114 Dinorwic, GWYNEDD. A cottage on the mountainside (*page 152*)
115 Near Harlech, GWYNEDD. Huge stone blocks and sturdy proportions give this hillside farmhouse its character (*page 158*)
116 Corris Uchaf, GWYNEDD. Quarrymen's cottages below the slate tips (*page 159*)
117 Blaenau Ffestiniogg, GWYNEDD. An industrial terrace in the mountains (*page 159*)

118

119

120

121

WALES

118 Abereiddi, DYFED. Whitewashed stone cottages with slurried roofs (*page 160*)
119 Garn Dolbenmaen. GWYNEDD. A primitive cottage made of boulders (*page 153*)
120 Rhosson, DYFED. The strange cylindrical chimney-stacks are a feature of the old farmhouses near St Davids (*page 161*)
121 Bontnewydd, GWYNEDD. Green igneous rocks and a slate porch (*page 153*)

122

123

124

125

WALES

122 Pen-y-Bont, CLWYD. Rubble walls and slate roofs in central Wales (*page 152*)
123 Near Carmarthen, DYFED. A whitewashed inland farm (*page 156*)
124 Berriew, POWYS. Houses in the Vale of Powys in the full black-and-white tradition of the English West Midlands (*page 161*)
125 Ffynnongroew, CLWYD. Northern coalmining villages look much like those in the Pennines (*page 162*)

localities the pink limestone is used for walling with red sandstone dressings, a practice which looks less well than when the pink limestone is used alone, as in the Ravensworth area. However, although the buildings in their general use of render and paint have affinities with those in the coastal strip, here the colours chosen are more restrained and sophisticated. Black is frequently used for window and door surrounds; browns, greys and dark greens too are employed to great effect [105].

Painted sandstone (Vale of Eden, Cumbria)

Further east the Pennines stretch northwards as far as the Tyne, with buildings not very different from those of the Yorkshire Dales further south. Throughout this part of the Pennines, the country becomes more austere, grander in scale; the hills seemingly higher and bleaker, with moorland tops rather than grass; the valleys less prosperous, more deserted. The stonework is darker and relics of the industrial past in the form of deserted workings and the remains of abandoned aqueducts, smelt mills and moorland chimneys are even more in

evidence than further south. Here the hills are of carboniferous limestone, interspersed on the west and in the centre with outcrops of igneous basalts and dolerites, which provide the strange alternation of calcareous and acid soils that seem to favour the splendid proliferation of wild flowers for which the northern Pennines are so famous; a region where, on these waterlogged fells, whole hillsides of kingcups, with scattered globe flowers and northern primroses, are considered normal.

In this grand and rather lonely landscape, with its natural beauties and its sad undertones of departed industrial activities, the vernacular buildings of the Pennines pass almost unnoticed. With their stone roofs, low in pitch, and built of dark brown rubble stone, these humble buildings fit perfectly into their landscape. Here there are few of the more opulent features seen further south, and stone-mullioned windows are seldom seen, for on the whole this part of England was developed far later, and such quasi-medieval left-overs were not part of the building vocabulary of the eighteenth-century settlers, farmers and miners who built the houses.

In the western part of the northern Pennines the pattern of farmhouse building is almost standard: two-storeyed buildings with the staircase stuck out at the back under an extended roof, the byre and barn attached in line, sometimes under a lower roof and sometimes under one long roof. Whitewashing is common among these upper dales [110], but further north and east, certainly below Middleton in Teesdale, the practice is far less common, and in Northumberland it is rare.

In all this area of the northern Pennines, huge sandstone roofing slabs are universal [109], but the sharp projecting kneelers, so typical of Yorkshire and Lancashire houses, are less often seen, for fewer houses in this area aspire to expensive parapets to their gables.

North of the Tyne lies the upland country of the Roman Wall. The pale green grass rolls away on either hand, dipping and surging in a long series of low-topped ridges like the waves of the sea [108]. Prosperous farms shelter in the little valleys leading down to the Tyne on the south, while northwards beyond the

Wall the land stretches emptily away in an infinity of rolling green grass, unbroken to the horizon and beyond, until the almost totally uninhabited forested uplands of Wark, Kielder and eventually the Cheviot Hills themselves are reached.

All around this huge empty region there are few villages but many hamlets; this is Border Country, reflecting in its layout and appearance the different pattern of development imposed by the years of Border raids and warfare which lasted until the eighteenth century.

A Border farmstead (Northumberland)

Typically, especially along the eastern and southern foothills of the Cheviots, the hamlets are arranged round a four-square eighteenth-century farmhouse; a large brown-stone, slate-roofed two-storey house, the hamlet comprising a cluster of farm buildings and cottages, roofed like the farmhouse in dark grey plain slates. The cottages are humble single-storey buildings in rows or terraces, built of the same stone.

In this part of the country, the stone is the Fell Sandstone, part of the carboniferous series surrounding the igneous lump of the Cheviot Hills. The farms here are all much of a pattern. They were built by the great landowners for their tenant farmers, as were the modest single-storey cottage rows for the labourers

A Northumberland cottage row

[107]. This uniformity, taken with the straight roads and regular planting pattern, gives the countryside an artificial appearance of having been organised from above rather than having evolved, like so much of England elsewhere.

The north-east part of the region comprises the generally low-lying coastal area bordering the North Sea. This is a wild and windswept tract of country, with sand dunes, waving marram grass and close-cropped thymy headlands. The huge medieval castles of Bamburgh with its village and Dunstanburgh in its wrecked isolation punctuate the lonely coastal scene. Houses are built of the dark grey limestone, sometimes spotted with black and pink stones, and here, as elsewhere along the East Coast, roofs are of pantiles. The buildings as a consequence have a strong affinity with all red pantiled stone buildings in their simple square shapes and bright, telling roofs. South of Bamburgh there is some play made with the variegated stone colours, which are used with great effect to contrast as corner-stones and walling, either dark walling and pale corners or vice versa. At Warkworth the grim grey sandstone is again in evidence both in the gaunt castle and in the surrounding houses. This sombre style of Northumbrian building has a classical simplicity, helped by the large square courses of the Fell Sandstone and the sandstone roofing of the older houses.

Further south towards Tyne and Wear, the coalfields have almost totally influenced the buildings and their landscape. The coal-bearing strata extend inland far south of Tyne and Wear, and this, together with the large industrial concentration whose influence spreads outwards from the iron, steel and ship-building activities of Cleveland, has given the whole of the eastern part of Durham a rough, industrial character that swamps that of its older and more attractive buildings and has spoiled much of the natural beauty of the countryside, perhaps nowhere more poignantly than along the coal-bound coast.

Between the Durham coalfields and the ironstone of the Cleveland Hills, from which Middlesborough gained its iron ore, lies the soft Triassic valley of the Tees, with a wide band of Magnesian Limestone forming the northern part of the valley.

Some of this pale creamy-white limestone can be seen at Heighington, and here, as along the coast, roofing is of pantiles, bright red for the most part, extending inland wherever water transport was available. Simple shaped buildings result, with parapetted gables in most cases; some have stone kneelers at the corners, but not nearly so universally as in Yorkshire. The small towns bordering the Tees, such as Barnard Castle and Gainford, show a strong influence from the neighbouring Yorkshire plain, and the houses have steeper pitched pantiled roofs with painted render or brown brickwork surrounding their square sash windows.

One of the most striking features of this northern region is the difference between the rich architectural expression of Cumbria and the aloof austerity of Northumberland and the Durham Dales. By contrast, the vernacular architecture of Wales, as we shall see in the next chapter, is surprisingly consistent.

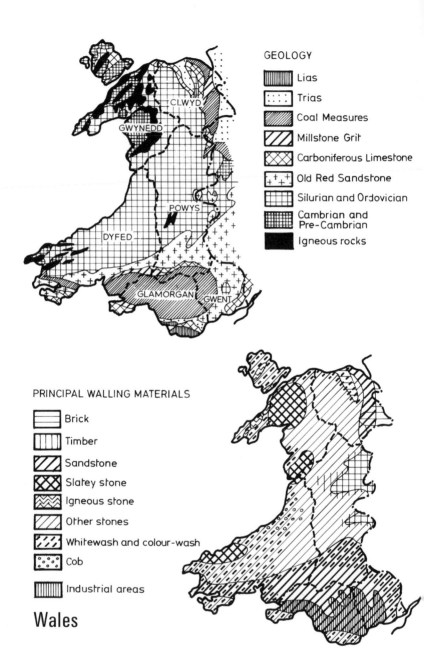

GEOLOGY

▥	Lias
⋰	Trias
▨	Coal Measures
▨	Millstone Grit
▨	Carboniferous Limestone
⁺⁺⁺	Old Red Sandstone
▦	Silurian and Ordovician
▥	Cambrian and Pre-Cambrian
■	Igneous rocks

CLWYD

GWYNEDD

POWYS

DYFED

GLAMORGAN   GWENT

PRINCIPAL WALLING MATERIALS

▤	Brick
⦀	Timber
▨	Sandstone
▨	Slatey stone
▨	Igneous stone
▨	Other stones
▨	Whitewash and colour-wash
⦂	Cob
⦀	Industrial areas

Wales

11. Wales
Gwynedd, Clwyd, Powys, Dyfed, Glamorgan and Gwent
Small White Houses, Mountains and Slate

Traditional buildings in Wales are nearly all built of stone.

The boundary between England and Wales follows roughly the edge of the mountains, with three notable exceptions where the mountains lie some way west of the border: in the south, all the eastern part of the county of Gwent, which is relatively low-lying although hilly; in the north, the coalmining and iron-producing areas of Clwyd in what used to be Flint and East Denbighshire; and in the centre, the broad vale of Powys—the valley of the Severn—which penetrates deep into central Wales. In all these comparatively lowland areas the style of building follows the traditions of the adjacent English counties more closely than it does those of Wales.

Most of the fascination of Wales lies in the dramatic mountains of Snowdonia, and a large part of their popularity lies in their apparent size. By some trick of the changing light, of the rainwashed air, now clear, now veiled in mist, or of the swiftly moving clouds that only half reveal the peaks and shadowy cwms, these comparatively modest Welsh crags are made to seem like great mountain ranges.

In the south-west, the St David's peninsula is by contrast low-lying, but again the conical rocky hills and tors, which stand up above the general level of the farms and fields like small islands, look in all but the clearest weather like sizeable mountains.

This air of apparent exaggeration in the natural features of the country is in direct contrast to its traditional architecture, whose principal characteristic is one of unassuming simplicity.

Between the mountains of the north-west and the rocky headlands of Dyfed—the two most spectacular regions of the country—lies central Wales, a very large highland area, sparsely populated and crossed by few roads. Here the hills, unlike the mountains of the north-west, are smooth, not jagged, and are generally a good deal lower. Furthermore, they all rise to much the same level, so that from any hilltop that raises its head a few hundred feet above its neighbours, the bare ridges can be seen receding in apparently endless succession, like waves of the sea.

South of the central mass, the Old Red Sandstone of the Brecon Beacons and of Fforest Fawr gives way southwards to the high Pennant sandstone moors heading-off the coalfields of South Wales, where the dark tips and long rows of terrace houses dominate the narrow, winding valleys.

But Wales is essentially rural; only in the extreme south and north has industry imposed a different way of life. There are few great wealthy farms, as in the English Midlands, the pattern generally being of small farms and crofts whose livelihood has derived from stock-raising and marketing, droving and hill farming. The result of this pattern of life on the buildings is obvious. Houses are small, cottages and small farmhouses are the rule [112, 114], spaced not far apart, but seldom clustered together in villages except in the coastal areas or where the English influence is most strongly felt, as in south Pembrokeshire and the Vale of Glamorgan as well as in eastern districts where perhaps the more prosperous way of life, due to the proximity of the Midlands markets, has penetrated across the border.

Wales underwent its great period of rebuilding very largely in the late eighteenth and nineteenth centuries [122], in contrast to most of England, whose great rebuilding period was the seventeenth century, and this goes a long way towards explaining the relative consistency of its vernacular architecture. Earlier houses were often built on too modest a scale to survive to-day, except where they have been converted into barns and byres, nor have rural communities expanded during the twentieth century to anything like the extent that they have in England.

The presence of so many Regency and Victorian-style buildings in North Wales is largely due to the appeal its scenery and unsophisticated rural way of life had for the romantics of the period, as well as to the development of the slate quarries at that time.

Although prosperity came to the rest of rural Wales rather slowly, and indeed the traditional small crofting and farming life continued alongside the industrial developments more or less undisturbed, there are very few farms and cottages that do not have late Georgian or Victorian improvements in the form of either extra rooms in the roof with dormers, a new front complete with sash windows or a total rebuild of everything except the massive chimney.

Geologically, by far the greater part of the Welsh central uplands are made of ancient Ordovician and Silurian rocks, all dark-toned, some hard and lumpy, some shaley and friable, some slatey, thin and hard. Greys, blacks and greenish tints predominate. In the north and extreme south-west the volcanic rocks produce a variety of strong colours with bright dark greens and reds [121], apparent more in field walls than in houses, which are seldom left unrendered or unpainted.

It would be tedious to differentiate area by area between the various sorts of rock encountered in Wales, for in fact these differences have remarkably little effect upon the building forms and techniques throughout the country. The only real difference made to the buildings by the type of rock used is one of surface treatment—thin, slatey rocks horizontally laminated; large, lumpy igneous rocks [119]; huge, rounded boulders from the glaciers; soft rocks that have to be rendered to keep the weather out, and so on.

With very few exceptions indeed, slate is the universal roofing material for the whole of Wales. The violent volcanic eruptions of Ordovician times that gave rise to the hard volcanic rocks of the north-west and the headlands around St David's, baked and squeezed the adjacent Ordovician and Cambrian shales and mudstones into slate.

Slate of the finest quality and in gigantic quantities occurs in Gwynedd and to a lesser extent both in quality and quantity in western Dyfed (the Pembrokeshire peninsula). Some more detailed account of this material is given later in the chapter when discussing roofs, for the influence of slate on the appearance of Welsh buildings and on the economy of the country can hardly be over-emphasised.

Coal is of course the other major mineral product of Wales. In the south the development of the coalfields is a familiar story; here the late nineteenth and twentieth centuries take over with a vengeance. Terraces of houses mount up one above another along the contours of the valleys or plunge vertiginously down the slopes, with roofs stepped in the steepest streets, but sloped parallel to the pavements (a more economical arrangement) wherever the gradient permits. All the earlier terraces are made of the dark-browny sandstone of the Coal Measures. The later

Terraces in the coalmining valleys (Glamorgan)

terraces are either wholly of brick or of stone with brick arches over doors and windows, striped in alternate dark and light bricks or painted in bright colours. Roofs are of slates from North Wales and paintwork on the universal sash windows is immaculate. Front doors are given special attention where establishing an individual identity is of the utmost importance in so uniform an environment. Some are grained and varnished, some are of glass with fanciful arrangements of glazing bars, and all are carefully painted. Neat lace curtains hang in every window, and front rooms, more often than not giving straight on to the pavement with no front gardens, are decorated with bright china vases and lovingly tended plants.

Although it would be interesting to examine in detail the building styles developed in the coalmining valleys, in a mainly rural region like Wales it is the farms and cottages of the countryside which are more important.

The typical Welsh farm stands isolated against its hill, a long line of farm buildings, with the house either at one end or neatly in the middle of the row, with its two chimneys and its door and windows symmetrically arranged. Older farmhouses and cottages, now well in the minority, are of one storey, some with bedrooms in the roof lit by slate gabled dormers added in the nineteenth century. These older buildings, in the rare cases where they have escaped the improvements of the last hundred and fifty years, display none of the symmetry imposed by late Georgian or Victorian taste but have their small, deep-set windows arranged seemingly at random, with the entrance between the house and byre in the long-house pattern.

Isolated mountain farm on Cader Idris (Gwynedd)

In these houses, the entrance doorway opened direct to a through passage which served the living-room on the one hand (through which the bedroom was reached) and the byre for the cattle on the other. The through passage was the feeding walk, so the animals' heads were facing the living-room, from which they could be seen—a friendly arrangement that must also have given to both parties the benefit of mutual warmth and a feeling of security. To-day the most notable characteristics of the Welsh farm are its neatness, cleanliness, careful upkeep and, in the vast majority, the tidiness and symmetry of its layout.

Whitewash, or less often colour-wash, is used in nearly all districts of Wales, though in some much more universally than in others, applied to rough stonework or render as an added protection from the weather, for appearance and for cleanliness [123]. Whitewashing year by year over the centuries has resulted in a build-up of material over the rough stonework which gives the older buildings their characteristic smothered texture—smooth and lumpy at the same time—for some of the underlying masonry is very rough indeed, since the builders had to cope with boulders and lumps of rock too hard to be cut; at best they could be broken and the pieces selected rather than shaped [113].

Whitewashed cottages (Dyfed)

In some farms of the south-west, farm outbuildings and the older side of the farmhouse facing the farmyard are white-washed, while the 'improved' front of the house, facing the road or garden, is left in plain stone, an arrangement which highlights the protective and hygienic function of the whitewash rather than its decorative qualities.

Whitewash is particularly popular in coastal districts, and in some, like Anglesey, the Lleyn Peninsula, north Pembroke (where in fact pink and ochre colour-wash is also popular) or the Gower, plain stone buildings are the exception. These areas seem to have remaining a greater proportion of the older stone buildings than is the case elsewhere in the region. Colour-wash is also a good deal used in central West Wales, particularly along the coast at such fishing villages as Aberarth or the more sophisticated eighteenth-century style port of Aberaeron, mostly built during the first part of the nineteenth century.

In the less mountainous parts of central West Wales, single-storey cottages built of cob can still be found, their thatched roofs now unhappily covered with corrugated iron, for the cost of upkeep of the thatch must be high. Even the corrugated iron looks quite well, painted black over the heavily whitewashed cob buildings. Although chimneys in these houses are usually of brickwork, they were originally constructed of lath and plaster, thatched on the outside, giving a curious and characteristic hump to the ridge at the junction of house and byre.

A cob cottage (north Dyfed)

In remote country districts, prosperous-looking Victorian or Georgian-type farmhouses can be seen standing beside a long row of outbuildings made of gigantic rough stones, and as often as not these comprise the original long-house, the living quarters (in the more primitive ones built without windows, and only with doorways) being now used as an extension to byre or barn. In the

Typical later farmhouse (Dyfed)

later farmhouses, slate-roofed porches are common, placed in the centre of the house front with a square-headed or arched entrance way. Chimneys are always placed at the ends of the house roof and, in southern counties, the one which serves the main downstairs room is nearly always a little bigger and more clumsily built than the other, almost certainly because it was the original and only chimney in the house, the other having been added in a neater and more prosperous age.

Roofs throughout Wales are almost invariably gabled, hips being practically unknown. Parapetted gables were common in the older houses, but roughly built like the main house walls [115]. Later improved roofs are more often taken across to form a verge. Roofs are low-pitched (35° to 40°), as suits the closely fitting Welsh slates, but not so low-pitched as the heavy sandstone roofs of the Welsh Marches or the Pennine moorlands. Eaves hardly overhang at all, a few inches at the most, and chimneys and walls are usually furnished with stepped slate weather-sheds, built into the masonry above the junction with the roof.

Slate roofs in Wales are of two sorts: the typical product of the nineteenth century industry of North Wales, and the rougher local product. The former provides a roof of neat, large rectangular slates laid in regular courses and split as thin as cardboard. It is a superfine material that in the hands of a skilled craftsman can be split and split again, without breaking, to an almost incredible thinness for what is after all a natural rugged rock. Such slates come from the world-famous quarries of Snowdonia.

Welsh slates are of variable colour, the most common being darkish purpley-grey or blue-grey, the standard product of the great quarries lying to the north-west of Snowdon at Penrhyn, Bethesda and Dinorwic. The Dorothea quarry, a vast pit in the ground near Nantlle, produced a quite bright, pinky-mauve slate. There are green bands in most quarries and the Ordovician mines and quarries of Corris [116] and Blaenau Ffestiniog produce a somewhat darker blue-black. Further south in Dyfed, the Rosebush quarry in the Prescelly Mountains at one time also produced a fine slate, but no quarry approaches the size and magnificence of the gigantic terraced excavations of Penrhyn.

Slates from these Welsh quarries covered the roofs of Victorian Britain and were exported all over the world from little ports like Portmadoc, Port Dinorwic and Newport near Fishguard. Their combined production at the peak of their prosperity was prodigious and there are in addition innumerable abandoned mines and quarries scattered all over Snowdonia. The remains of these quarries, light railways, tips and dressing sheds, all grown over with grass and bilberries, make a striking and romantic contribution to the high valleys of North Wales.

The houses of slate quarrymen are like quarrymen's houses anywhere in Britain, built of magnificent pieces of stone, but all on a modest scale. Sometimes in terraces, sometimes individually, the two-storeyed houses are typical examples of nineteenth-century artisans' dwellings [117]. The comparatively

Quarry cottage (Gwynedd)

rough walling of these cottages is occasionally offset by an elaborate porch, canopy or pair of gate-posts, in smoothly finished purple slate, as examples of the owner's craftsmanship and perhaps his status in the quarry. The slate field boundary fences made with long staves or fangs of slate, driven into the ground and wired together, are a striking feature of slate-producing areas and give the neighbourhood a curiously improvised appearance. Later houses, as in Corris near Machynlleth, are built of sawn quarry-waste, but unlike similarly built Lakeland houses, all the stones are carefully flush-jointed in mortar.

Locally produced slates can be seen throughout the north of Pembroke, on many of the buildings in the Lleyn Peninsula and on Anglesey, as well as in central Wales. The slates are generally thicker, smaller and rougher than the fine product of the big quarries and in coastal districts the roofs are usually slurried over with cement mortar. In the old days, the slates were jointed with lime mortar to keep out driving rain and were plastered underneath between the roof joists. In exposed situations, particularly around St David's, the roofs are held down with wires which are stretched across the house over the ridge and secured at the eaves. The wires are then mortared in and slurried over to form roughly parallel ridges down the slope of the roof about four or five feet apart [118], the ridges giving a distinctive and not unattractive appearance to the grey roofs, which just show the pattern of the tiling through their blanket or mortar. Occasionally, enthusiastic whitewashers will include the roof with the walls, the all-white house creating a very striking effect indeed [113].

Ridged and slurried roofs (Dyfed)

Around St David's a few of the oldest farmhouses have a lean-to roof on the entrance side of the house through which grows, beside the arched doorway, a massive side chimney. The houses have been sadly altered but were originally of one storey, the lean-to being a sort of aisle with its roof at a slightly lower pitch than the main roof. But it is not only the unusual arrangement of aisle and side chimney that is striking; above eaves-level the stack is built up as a huge, tapering cylinder [120]. Other round chimneys can be seen in some areas of south Pembrokeshire (as well as in Somerset and Cumbria), but none so large. Various

An ancient farmhouse (near St David's)

theories have been advanced for this phenomenon, as for example that it is an architectural fashion introduced by the Flemish immigrants who were invited to settle in Pembrokeshire and in the Vale of Glamorgan by Henry I in the early twelfth century; or that it is an architectural survival from the Norman romanesque, as seen in some larger houses in the area. However that may be, these are only local variations on the vernacular style of the region and cannot be in any way described as typical.

Along the boundary between England and Wales, the local buildings are similar to those in England. The valley of the Severn and its tributaries penetrate far into the hills of central Wales and all along the valley bottoms older farms can be found, few and far between though they are to-day, built in the full black-and-white tradition of the English West Midlands [124]. Here roofs are of Welsh slates, which gives these houses a slightly more local flavour than if they were roofed in sandstone slabs as in England. Sandstone roofs are however often seen in Gwent, the eastern two-thirds of which is on the Old Red Sandstone formation, as is neighbouring Herefordshire. Buildings in this part of Wales are built in the warm pinkish-grey lichened sandstone of the district—not of timber, as in the Vale of Powys and north Herefordshire.

The buildings of the coalmining and industrial part of northern Clwyd are very similar to their Pennine counterparts, although less flamboyantly grim and far less blackened by smoke [125], and it is not until the Clwyd itself is crossed that the buildings in this part of Wales assume any very distinctively Welsh appearance.

One of the most striking of all areas in the region is the island of Anglesey. Built of exceedingly ancient rocks and steeped in history and legend, its heavily whitewashed older houses, with their slurried grey roofs, antique and often irregular, appeal strongly to the imagination. The countryside is low-lying, with few rocky hills, and is gentle by comparison with the mountains of North Wales, which form the splendid scenic backdrop to every southward view in the island. Although much nineteenth-century rebuilding and alteration took place, particularly after the construction of Telford's main road to Holyhead, many earlier houses remain virtually unchanged. These older buildings in Anglesey are often of one storey [111], and even the two-storey houses seem to crouch low to the ground. They all have deeply recessed windows in their thick and brilliantly white-washed stone walls.

One other area of Wales must be mentioned, and that lies at the extreme opposite end of the country. South of the South Wales coalfields lies the little Vale of Glamorgan, rural, prosperous and largely unaffected by the industrial concentration so near at hand. Houses in the Vale are grouped in villages, much as in England. Cottages are built of grey Liassic limestone or the paler carboniferous limestone, often rendered and nearly always whitewashed, the older cottages being sometimes still thatched. The grouping of the cottages in the villages, the thatch and the whitewash, together contribute towards the English atmosphere in this small part of Wales, a cosy, rural atmosphere somewhat alien to that of Wales as a whole.

We have not made a serious attempt to describe the geology of Wales in any detail. It has been called a geologist's paradise, but the many changes in the underlying rocks, although they have created the country's relief and have profoundly influenced its economy, have made surprisingly little difference to the appearance of its older traditional buildings from one end of the country to the other.

Illustrated Glossary

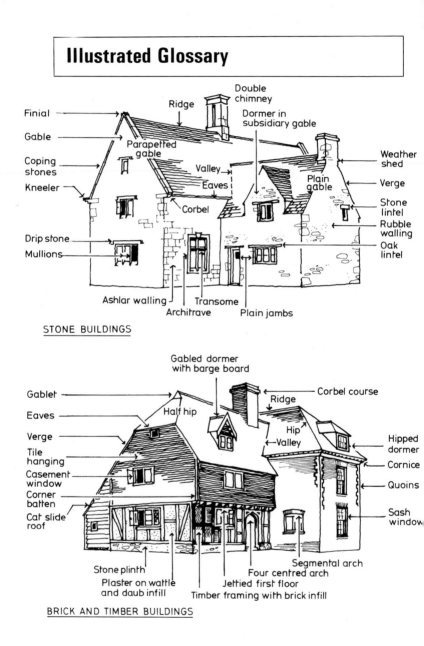

Finial

Gable

Coping stones

Kneeler

Drip stone

Mullions

Ridge

Parapetted gable

Valley

Eaves

Corbel

Double chimney

Dormer in subsidiary gable

Plain gable

Weather shed

Verge

Stone lintel

Rubble walling

Oak lintel

Ashlar walling

Architrave

Transome

Plain jambs

STONE BUILDINGS

Gabled dormer with barge board

Gablet

Eaves

Verge

Tile hanging

Casement window

Corner batten

Cat slide roof

Half hip

Corbel course

Ridge

Hip

Valley

Hipped dormer

Cornice

Quoins

Sash window

Stone plinth

Plaster on wattle and daub infill

Segmental arch

Four centred arch

Jettied first floor

Timber framing with brick infill

BRICK AND TIMBER BUILDINGS

Short Bibliography

General Books

M. W. Barley, *The House and Home*, Vista Books, London, 1963

H. Braun, *Old English Houses*, Faber, London, 1962

M. S. Briggs, *The English Farmhouse*, Batsford, London, 1938

R. W. Brunskill, *Illustrated Handbook of Vernacular Architecture*, Faber, London, 1971; new edition, 1978

A. Clifton-Taylor, *The Pattern of English Building*, Batsford, London, 1962; new edition, Faber, London, 1972

O. Cook and E. Smith, *English Cottages and Farmhouses*, Thames and Hudson, London, 1954

A. Henderson, *The Family House in England*, Phoenix, London, 1964

E. C. Holmes and S. R. Jones, *Village Homes of England*, The Studio, 1912

S. R. Jones, *English Village Homes*, Batsford, London, 1936

E. Mercer, *English Vernacular Houses*, Royal Commission on Historical Monuments, HMSO, London, 1975

J. Prizeman, *Your House—the Outside View*, Hutchinson, London, 1975

T. West, *The Timber-framed House in England*, David and Charles, Newton Abbot, 1971

Regional Books

R. W. Brunskill, *Vernacular Architecture of the Lake Counties*, Faber, London, 1974

V. M. and F. J. Chesher, *The Cornishman's House*, Bradford Barton, Truro, 1968

I. C. Peate, *The Welsh House*, Brython Press, Liverpool, 1940

P. Smith, *Houses of the Welsh Countryside*, Royal Commission on Historical Monuments, HMSO, London, 1976

R. B. Wood-Jones, *Traditional Domestic Architecture of the Banbury Region*, Manchester University Press, 1963

Books on Allied Subjects
W. G. Hoskins, *The Making of the English Landscape*, Hodder and Stoughton, London, 1955; Penguin, Harmondsworth, 1970
A. E. Trueman, *Geology and Scenery in England and Wales*, Gollancz, London, 1938; Penguin, Harmondsworth, 1949

Index